HUMMINGBIRD RIDGE

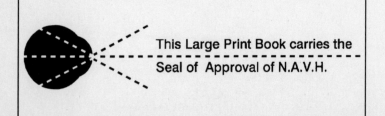

This Large Print Book carries the
Seal of Approval of N.A.V.H.

HUMMINGBIRD RIDGE

MARGARET NAVA

THORNDIKE PRESS
A part of Gale, Cengage Learning

GALE
CENGAGE Learning

Detroit • New York • San Francisco • New Haven, Conn • Waterville, Maine • London

GALE
CENGAGE Learning™

LIBRARY OF CONGRESS CATALOGING-IN-PUBLICATION DATA

Nava, Margaret M., 1942–
　　Hummingbird Ridge / by Margaret Nava. — Large print ed.
　　　p. cm. — (Thorndike Press large print clean reads)
　　Originally published: Memphis, TN: Bell Bridge Books, c2009.
　　ISBN-13: 978-1-4104-3046-5
　　ISBN-10: 1-4104-3046-4
　　1. Older women—Fiction. 2. Self-realization in women—Fiction.
　　3. West Virginia—Fiction. 4. Large type books. I. Title.
　　PS3614.A925H86 2010
　　813'.6—dc22　　　　　　　　　　　　　　　　　　　2010021420

Published in 2010 by arrangement with BelleBooks, Inc.

Printed in the United States of America
1 2 3 4 5 6 7 14 13 12 11 10

To all of Angela's friends, young and old, near and far. Thank you for loving her.

1
A New Life

A gentle breeze ruffled Angela's dress as she and Gilberto walked across the white sand beach. Her cherished friend, Katherine, helped choose that dress. It was shell-pink chiffon with a Battenberg lace insert at the bodice and a handkerchief hem that barely brushed the top of her ankles. With delicate pink flowers in her hair and a simple gold cross around her neck, she looked and felt beautiful.

Even though it was December, the sun shone bright and the sky was almost cloudless. Hurricane season was long gone and the holidays were just around the corner. Last year she spent the holidays at a boat parade and a basketball game, the year before she had been in Indiana. She'd come so far since then. She'd given up her job, driven herself all the way to Florida, met some strange and wonderful people, lived through a hurricane, cut all ties with her ex-husband and, now, was just about to start a brand-new life. If anyone back in Indiana had told her she was capable of doing half those things, she would have questioned their sanity.

"Are you sure you want to do this?" whispered Gilberto.

"Positive." Angela squeezed Gilberto's hand and gazed into his eyes. "I've never been surer of anything in my life." She had come so close to losing him. Now, she would never let him go.

Their friend Steve stood waiting in a small white gazebo under the palm trees. Instead of his usual turtleneck or muscle shirt, he wore a black clerical shirt and stiff white collar, vestiges of his days as a Catholic priest. He smiled as Angela and Gilberto approached and motioned for them to kneel when they entered the gazebo. Placing his hands on their heads, he began the ceremony.

"Heavenly Father, our hearts are filled with great happiness on this day as Angela and Gilberto come before you pledging their hearts and lives to one another. Grant that they may ever be true and loving, living together in such a way as to never bring shame or heartbreak into their marriage. Temper their hearts with kindness and understanding. Rid them of all pretense and jealousy. Help them to remember to be each other's sweetheart, helpmate, best friend and guide, so that together they may meet the cares and problems of life bravely. May the home they are creating today truly be a place of love and harmony where your Spirit is always present."

Looking out around the gazebo, Angela noticed her brother Tony and his wife Fran sitting on linen-covered folding chairs. Steve's wife, Monica, was next to them, and Katherine and her husband Mongo were directly behind. There were about twenty other people in the small group, including Gilberto's bocce friends, Katherine's Foxy Ladies and Mrs. Snodgrass, the woman from the rundown trailer park, who was escorted by Gilberto's long-lost nephew. Everyone was smiling and seemed to be wearing their Sunday-best clothes. Even Tony. It made her feel good to know she had so many caring friends.

Steve extended his hands as Angela and Gilberto rose to their feet. Then, sounding very much like a protective father, he continued. "Gilberto Fontero, in front of God and all these people, do you take Angela Dunn to be your wife?"

"I do."

Smiling at Angela, he asked, "Angela Dunn, in front of God and all these people, do you take Gilberto Fontero to be your husband?"

"I do."

"Gilberto, is there something you would like to say to Angela?"

"*Sì,* there is. Angela, on this wondrous day, I take you to be my wife and my friend, the one I will live with, dream with and laugh with. You have brought sunlight and joy into my life. I hope that I can bring happiness to your life. From now until forever, I will cherish you. I will look with joy down the path of our tomorrows knowing we will walk it together side by side, hand-in-hand and heart-to-heart. And I will love you for as long as we both shall live." Gilberto trembled as he placed a simple gold band on Angela's finger.

"Angela, is there something you would like to say to Gilberto?"

"Yes, there is. Gilberto, when we met, my life was filled with confusion and despair. You showed me the true meaning of love and helped me learn to trust again. I love you above all others and treasure our friendship as a precious gift. I promise to stand beside you in sickness or health, in times of prosperity or hardship, in peace or in turmoil, and I promise to love you as long as we both shall live." Angela smiled as she placed a matching gold band on Gilberto's finger.

"Angela and Gilberto, in as much as the two of you have agreed to live together in Holy Matrimony and have promised your love for each other by these vows and the giving of rings, I now declare you to be husband and wife. May the Lord bless you and keep you. May He make His face to shine upon you and be gracious unto you. May He lift up His countenance unto to you and give you peace. Gilberto, you may kiss your bride. Angela, you may kiss your husband."

Gil and Angela kissed as Steve concluded the ceremony. "Ladies and Gentlemen, it is with great pleasure that I present to you Mr. and Mr. Gilberto Fontero."

Tony was the first to jump out of his chair and rush toward Angela. "Guess I can quit worrying about you now," he beamed.

Katherine poked him in the ribs. "What were you worried about? That girl always knew what she wanted. She just didn't know how to get it. That's where I came in."

"Oh, so you're saying you're the one that got Angela and Gil together?" Tony's grin dissolved into laughter.

"OK, you two," scolded Monica, "cut it out. This is Gil and Angela's day, don't ruin it."

"Nothing could ruin it," shouted Angela. "I'm so happy I could kiss them both." She grabbed Tony and Katherine and planted a big, wet kiss on each of them.

"Yuk," sputtered Katherine. "You haven't been kissing that crazy dog of yours lately, have you?"

Angela gave Katherine a friendly shove then turned to the rest of her guests. "Gil and I are so grateful you were able to join us today that we'd like to invite you back to his, sorry, *our* home for a little celebration. Nothing fancy, just some finger food and cake."

"What?" protested Tony. "No beer?"

"No," replied Gilberto. "But we have champagne punch."

"Whoop-dee-doo," scoffed Tony. "Sounds like a fun party."

Back at Gilberto's trailer, several tables were covered in white tablecloths and laid out with Italian canapés, pâté and caviar on crostini, antipasto, imported cheeses, a fresh fruit tower, assorted Italian breads, a three-tiered red velvet wedding cake laced with raspberry preserves and covered in cream cheese frosting, and a huge cut-glass punch bowl filled with champagne, orange juice and delicate white magnolias.

"Gee, I'm glad you didn't fuss," joked Katherine.

"Nothing is too good for our friends," replied Gilberto.

"Speaking of which," boasted Katherine, "Mongo and I have a little something for you."

"It's not rabbits, is it?" Monica frowned and shook her head. "No, it is not," barked Katherine. "Why would we give them rabbits?"

"I don't know," mocked Monica. "Maybe because you have too many?" Right after she and Steve announced they were buying a farm in West Virginia, Mongo started raising rabbits to give to them as a housewarming gift. The hurricane altered his plans, but maybe he'd started over.

"Shall I say grace?" interrupted Steve.

"Please," muttered Tony. "I'm about to starve."

"Dear Lord, we thank you for bringing our two friends together and showing them that all things are possible with you. We also thank you for this beautiful day and for the food we are about to receive. May your sun always shine on Gilberto and Angela and may their table always be filled with your goodness. Amen."

"Amen," exclaimed Tony. "Let's eat."

"Wait a minute," objected Katherine. "We haven't given them our gift yet."

"Oh, all right," grumbled Tony. "But make it quick."

Mongo dragged a large box out from under the picnic table. It looked like he was having trouble moving it so Katherine ran to his rescue. "Ever since we got married, he's been acting tired. Think I'm too much woman for him?"

"Katherine, please," laughed Angela. "You're in mixed company."

"Oh, yeah," teased Katherine, "like Father Steve and Sister Monica don't know what I'm talking about."

"Hurry up, Angela," snickered Steve. "Open the box before she gets too graphic."

Gilberto helped Mongo lift the box to the table then he and Angela removed the bow and wrapping paper. "Wonder what it could be?" asked Angela.

"We will know in a minute." Gilberto sliced the box open with a pocketknife.

"Balls?" questioned Angela when she looked inside.

"Not just balls," corrected Katherine. "They're bocce balls and they're personalized with your names. See? This one says

Angela and this one says *Gil*." She held up two balls for everyone to see.

"Thank you so much," stammered Gilberto. "I am sure they will be very useful."

"Sure," giggled Katherine, "when you get tired playing bocce ball you can throw them at each other."

"We'd never do that," chuckled Angela. "And the game is called *Bocce,* not *bocce ball*."

"Excuse me, Mrs. Fontero. I stand corrected." Katherine's eyes glistened as she beamed at her friend.

Angela thought back to the day she first met Katherine. Even though the redheaded woman was loud and brash, there had been an immediate connection. She offered friendship to Angela when she needed it most. She shared her life with Angela and made her feel like family. She was everything Angela was not. Katherine was adventurous, Angela was timid. Katherine was boisterous, Angela was quiet. Katherine was a flirt, Angela was not. It was those differences that made them friends, and it was those differences that would keep them friends.

Tony cleared his throat. "Well, as long as we're giving gifts, here's one from Fran and me." He reached into his pocket, pulled out two small boxes, handed one to Angela and the other to Gilberto.

Angela opened her box first. Inside was a small gold charm and chain. The charm was in the shape of a little girl on a bicycle. Tears came to her eyes when she looked at her brother.

"Just in case you need to find your way back home." Tony took a deep breath then nodded his head toward Gilberto. "Now open yours, Gil."

Gilberto opened his box and found another charm, this one in the shape of a little boy pushing a little girl on a bicycle.

"In case she ever needs help," mumbled Tony.

Several people sniffled and blew their noses.

Monica broke the mood. "We didn't bring our gift because it wouldn't fit in a box."

Angela borrowed Gilberto's handkerchief and wiped her tears. "You and Steve drove all the way down here just so he could preside over our wedding. You don't have to give us anything else."

"But we want to." Steve cleared his throat and hugged his wife. "Monica and I would like the two of you to spend your honeymoon on our farm. You can go hiking, do some bird watching, pick black walnuts or maybe even go fishing. There's an old trailer on the property. It's not much to look at, but it'll keep you warm and dry. You can just kick back, relax and enjoy yourselves. Monica made me promise not to bug you too much. With all the work she makes me do, you probably won't even know I'm around."

"That is so generous," replied Gilberto. "But we would be an imposition."

"No, you would not," argued Monica. "In fact, if you want to know the truth, I need someone to show me what to do with all those rabbits Mongo gave me."

"How many did he give you?" asked Angela.

"Too many," replied Monica.

"Well, as long as you think we could help . . ."

"You would be a big help," admitted Steve. "Please say yes."

Gilberto and Angela looked at each other, smiled, and replied in unison, "We accept."

2
THIS OLD FARM

Steve and Monica's farm sat deep within a hollow nine miles from the closest blacktop road. To reach it, Angela and Gilberto had to drive down a single-track dirt road, snake around rocky hilltops, navigate three low-water crossings and pull to the side whenever a Jeep or truck approached from the opposite direction. Most of the homes at the head of the hollow were relatively new and cared for but those further in looked like something out of *The Grapes of Wrath.* One barn was so run down, it looked like the only thing holding it up was a faded chewing tobacco sign painted on its side.

Beyond a fork in the road, there was what appeared to be an old ghost town. In his letter describing how to find the farm Steve explained that this area had once been a prosperous mining camp but when the coal ran out, the miners left and squatters moved into the abandoned buildings. Angela found it hard to believe families were living in ramshackle schoolhouses, stores and saloons but that's exactly what they were doing. What if they were making moonshine? She began to question the wisdom of spending a honeymoon in West Virginia.

Just about the time she made up her mind to ask Gil to turn around, there it was. One hundred acres of rolling pastures, verdant bottomlands and steep hills covered with what Steve identified as black walnut trees, mulberry bushes, wild roses and dogwood. Gizmo stuck his head out the window and breathed in the amazing scents. A 1940-ish red tractor stuck halfway out of a not-quite-dilapidated shed and a flock of chickens pecked at bugs and inchworms that crawled around a dried-up vegetable patch. Perched high on a hill, a two-story, more-gray-than-white, clapboard house overlooked the river that ran through the property. Across the wooden bridge that spanned the river was a tear-shaped, rusted trailer and two weathered Adirondack chairs placed near a rock-rimmed fire pit. Angela visualized herself sitting in one of those chairs watching deer, squirrels or maybe even river otters as they made their way to the water. It was wild. It was wonderful. It was more than she ever imagined.

Monica came running from the house even before Gil had time to park the car. "I've been waiting all day for you," she shrieked. "I began to think you weren't coming."

The ex-nun's desperate tone made Angela wonder if she was lonely. Hadn't she made any friends yet?

"Well, we're here now," chirped Angela as she and Gilberto got out of the car. She arched her back and rubbed her neck. It had been a long trip but Gilberto insisted on doing all the driving. Sometimes he acted more like fifty than eighty.

"Come inside," urged Monica. "I've got some lemonade in the cooler. It isn't fresh-squeezed, but you're not in Florida anymore, so you'll just have to make do."

The cooler? Was Monica already picking up the local jargon?

"Welcome to Wildwood Acres," Steve pushed the screen door open and joined his wife.

"Wildwood Acres?" questioned Gilberto. "And do you call your church the Church in the Wildwood?"

"How'd you guess? Actually, the people in the hollow gave it that name because it's surrounded by so many trees. Guess they took it from that old hymn. I liked it so much I decided to use it for the farm. Think God will forgive me?"

"He might," scolded Monica. "But I won't unless you go inside and get that lemonade. Gil and Angela have been driving all day. They must be parched. And get some water for that dog. He looks like he could use it."

"I will help," volunteered Gilberto.

"Me, too." Angela tied Gizmo to the car hoping he wouldn't take it with him if he spotted something he wanted to chase. Even though the dog was half-blind, his nose still worked and he would probably end up in the next county before anyone could catch him.

Steve and Gilberto were already inside when Angela and Monica entered the kitchen.

"Oh my gosh," exclaimed Angela. "Look at that refrigerator."

"It's not a refrigerator," corrected Monica. "It's a cooler. It doesn't even get cold enough to make ice."

"Isn't it great?" Steve patted the top of the refrigerator as if it were his favorite hunting dog. "It came with the house."

"My mother had one just like it when we first came to the United States." Gilberto ran his hand affectionately down the side of the monitor-top refrigerator. Looking at the legs, he noticed the foot pedal. "If I am not mistaken, I believe my father called that a knee-buster."

"No kidding?" Steve laughed. "That's exactly what happened the first time I tried to use it. What's it for?"

"Back in the days when these were popular, women stayed home and raised chickens and cows. When they brought the eggs and milk into the house, their hands were usually full. The pedal was put there so they could open the refrigerator door without having to put anything down."

"Clever," replied Steve.

"Check out the stove, Gil." Angela pointed across the room at a forty-inch-wide, double oven, double broiler O'Keefe & Merit range. "It even has a built-in griddle."

"I found that at the trading post in town," boasted Steve. "It was a real bargain. Only twenty bucks. One of the neighbors restored it for me. Pretty neat, huh?"

"Neat my eye," disagreed Monica. "I wanted a real stove but no, Mr. Oldies but Goodies here has to go out and buy a fifty-year-old eyesore. He even tried to talk me into a beat-up old wringer-washer, but I put my foot down on that one."

"But honey, I thought you liked it." Steve tried to kiss his wife's cheek but she pushed him away.

"Get the lemonade," she demanded.

"Yes, dear." Steve grinned and did as ordered.

"Are you okay, Monica?" Angela thought she seemed a little out of sorts.

Monica frowned. "Yeah. It's just that people around here are pretty clannish and standoffish. All except J.B. Now there's a character I could do without."

"Who is J.B?" asked Gilberto.

"J.B. Walton," replied Steve. "He lives up the road from us."

"Like in John Boy?" Angela giggled.

"Exactly." Monica rolled her eyes.

"Now, come on hon, there's nothing wrong with J.B."

"Really? Then why won't he come to church on Sunday?"

"A lot of people in the hollow don't come," argued Steve.

"As if I didn't notice." Monica's face looked like she had just bitten into a green persimmon.

"Are you having trouble getting people to come to the church?" asked Gilberto.

"Trouble's not the word." Monica snatched the pitcher from Steve's hand and filled everyone's glass with lukewarm lemonade.

Steve tried to smile. "Right now only two or three people show up but I'm sure that will change."

"Why do you think that is?" asked Gilberto.

"It's probably just that we're new. People who have lived here a long while don't take kindly to strangers."

"Good grief. Now you're even talking like J.B." Monica turned her back, grabbed a dishcloth and furiously rubbed the kitchen counter. Angela wasn't sure she was crying but she thought she heard a sniffle.

Steve went to his wife and tried to console her. "He'll come around, hon. Just wait and see."

"Oh yeah? Then why did he say it would be a cold day in hell before he let anyone in his family walk into any do-gooder's church?"

"He called you do-gooders?" Angela once thought the same thing but never had the nerve to say it.

"And worse." Monica finally broke into tears.

Steve explained that most of the people in the hollow were brought up in what he called 'that old time religion.' "They're used to revivals, getting their sins washed away in the blood, and ministers that preach hellfire and brimstone. Monica and I tried to show them the gentler side of religion. Obviously, we failed."

"So what are you going to do?" asked Gilberto.

"I don't know. Just keep trying and hope for the best I guess."

Steve's courage impressed Angela. Aside from being drop dead gorgeous, the man was a rock. He had been that way in Florida and he hadn't changed since moving to West Virginia. If anything, he was even stronger and better looking. "Is there anything we can do?" she asked.

"Yeah. Pray for us. A lot." Steve laughed and kissed his wife on the cheek. This time, she didn't push him away.

Drying her eyes, Monica straightened her back and lifted her chin "Listen. You two are probably tired, so how about Steve takes you down to the trailer, you rest up a bit and then come back for dinner around six?"

"We'd like to take you out for dinner," offered Angela.

"There's no place to go," whined Monica. "Besides, they're talking about rain, and you don't want to be caught out on that road when it rains."

"Why not?" asked Gilberto.

"Because you might not get back," replied

Steve. "Remember all those low-water crossings on the way up? They were only a couple inches deep when you crossed them, but when it rains they can go to a couple of feet deep in minutes. I heard that a guy got stuck in one last year during a rainstorm and the water got so deep, so fast, that it washed him and his car five miles downstream before he could bat an eyelash."

"Who told you that?" sneered Monica. "J.B.?"

"Well, yes, but . . ."

"Never mind, just take Gil and Angela down to the trailer and help them get settled."

"Yes, dear."

Although the outside of the trailer looked like it hadn't seen paint in forty years, the inside was spotless. The bed, which took up half the interior, was covered with an embroidered white quilt and matching pillows. Lace curtains hung on the window behind a bent-twig rocker and a small table sat in one of the corners. On the table was a box of chocolate candy, a porcelain bowl and a pitcher. There was no radio, no television and no electricity. The only concession to the twenty-first century was a battery-operated lantern and a tatty-looking porta-potty.

"I love it," exclaimed Angela. "It'll be our little cocoon. We can just curl up and eat chocolate for a whole week." She hugged Gilberto.

"Well don't get too comfortable," warned Steve. "I think Monica's got big plans for you."

"Like what?" asked Gilberto.

"I'm not sure, but knowing her it'll probably be something exhausting. Now don't forget. Dinner is at six."

After stowing their suitcases, changing clothes and taking Gizmo for a long walk along the river, Angela and Gilberto made their way across the bridge and up to Steve and Monica's house. It was starting to get dark but the soft glow of candles on the dining room table led the way. When Steve opened the door, the smells of fried chicken and apple pie reminded Angela she hadn't eaten since noon.

"Hope you made extra," she announced. "I'm hungry enough to eat a horse."

"Sorry. No horses," laughed Steve. "Will chicken do?" He showed Angela and Gilberto into the dining room and introduced several people already gathered around the table. "This is Sharon and Randy Schuster and over there are Pam and J.B. Walton. Everyone, this is Gil and Angela Fontero.

They're on their honeymoon."

"Honeymoon?" Pam's forehead furrowed. "In this old holler?"

"Sure, why not?" asked Angela. "We live in Florida and thought it would be nice to get away from all the traffic and crowds."

"You'll do that, alright," replied Sharon. "Fact is, if you see any traffic down the end'a this here road, you'll knowed someone be lost. No one never comes down here lest they got good reason."

"Really?" asked Gilberto.

"Oh, yeah," replied Steve. "The road ends just beyond our house and the only people I've seen come this far are hunters. In case you didn't notice, my mailbox is a mile away. Even the postman won't come out here."

Angela turned toward Monica. "Does that bother you?"

"No," muttered Monica. "Not that."

Steve said grace, Monica passed the food and everyone settled in to the serious business of eating. When the meal was over and Monica was handing out slices of warm apple pie, J.B. asked if Steve knew anything about the farm's original owners.

"Just some rumors," replied Steve.

"Like what?" asked Angela.

Steve opened his mouth as if to say some-

28

thing but J.B. interrupted and started telling the story himself. "Sometime in the early forties, a man named Jake Withers bought this here farm. He raised pigs, grew some corn and cut timber for a nearby lumberyard. You know, the usual stuff."

Pam crossed her arms and sighed as if she'd heard the story a million times.

"Jake's wife, Bertha was her name, was in charge of the pigs. Every day she cleaned out their pen and made sure they had enough corn and clean hay. She loved those pigs and treated them like children. Even gave them names. As far as anyone could tell, Jake and Bertha Withers lived a happy and peaceful life." J.B. picked his pie up with his fingers and stuffed it into his mouth.

"As if that's possible in these boonies," mumbled Monica.

After licking his fingers and wiping his mouth on his sleeve, J.B. continued his story. "So it seems some men, I think they called 'em *landmen* back then, came up from Charleston one day to talk to Jake about drilling fer oil on his property. They told him they didn't want his land, just the oil under it and that they'd pay him a dollar an acre plus two cents for every barrel of oil they pulled outta it. Now Jake, he was a good man but he was also sort 'a lazy, so when those Charleston men told him he could make money without lifting a finger, why he jumped at the chance. The oil company put in'a bunch of wells, including the one up on the hill, and within four or five years, well, Jake he was rich. He quit cutting timber, let the weeds take over his fields and sold the pigs."

"But Bertha loved those pigs." Angela wondered what she would do if Gil ever sold Gizmo.

"That she did," replied J.B. "Now folks around here never thought Bertha Withers had both oars in the water, if you know what I mean, but that's a whole nother story. Anyways, when Jake sold those pigs, they say Bertha kind'a lost it. Guess she figured she could coax her beloved oinkers back with food cuz she went out every day and put down fresh hay and corn. But them pigs never showed up. One day, Withers found her lying dead in the pigpen."

"Poor woman." Angela took a bite of her pie. The apples were firm but juicy and the spices were perfection. She'd have to ask Monica for the recipe.

"Withers missed his wife so much that he took up where she left off. Just like her, he went out every day and put out food for

30

them pigs. Of course, them non-existent ham bones never got benefit of all that food but the local deer and wild dogs knew where to go for a good meal. Those animals must have thought it was the greatest thing since sliced bread but everyone in the hollow started complaining that deer were raiding their gardens and dogs were killing their chickens. Withers just ignored them."

J.B reached for another piece of pie but Pam slapped his hand.

"That winter turned out to be a bad one — lots of ice and snow. Even though no one saw Withers for a couple of weeks they didn't worry about him none because they reckoned he was snowbound. When he didn't show up at the feed store for his monthly supply of pig feed, a couple of them went out to check on him. They found him dead in the snow with his arms wrapped around that old well up on the hill."

"That's horrible." Angela wondered if J.B. was telling the truth or pulling her leg.

"True. But here's where things gets really squirrelly." J.B. had that weird look people always get when they're telling a far-fetched story. "Both Withers and his wife are buried in an old cemetery on the backside of this property but every once in a while someone spots Jake walking around in the woods. The

31

Johnsons out on Round Knob saw him two winters ago and old man Scruggs down in Stringtown says he saw him down by his pigpen last spring. Scruggs says he even caught a glimpse of him once up near Steve's TV antenna. Maybe he wanted to come visit his old farm."

"Yeah, right," laughed Angela. "Like this farm is haunted?"

"You never know." J.B. flashed a sinister grin.

"Well, I don't think anyone can top that," announced Steve. "So what say we call it a night? It's been a long day and Gil and Angela need some rest."

"Oh, yeah. Honeymooners . . ." J.B. laughed.

"Go home, J.B." insisted Monica.

"Yes, ma'am." He obeyed but grabbed another piece of pie on his way out.

Before settling in for the night, Angela and Gilberto took two blankets from inside the trailer and headed for the Adirondack chairs.

"It is so quiet here, I can hear my own breathing," whispered Gilberto.

"It's not as quiet as you think," replied Angela. "Hear that hoot, hoot, hoot?"

"Is that an owl?

"A great horned owl. And that high

squawking bark? That's a night heron. I'm not sure if it's a yellow-crowned or a black-crowned, but either way, it's a night heron."

"How do you know?" asked Gilberto.

"We had all sorts of birds back in Indiana. Even when I was a kid, I'd go out at night and listen to the night birds. Tony bought me a little tape recorder for my fifteenth birthday and I used it to record their songs. Then I went to my biology teacher and she identified them for me."

"What about that?" Gilberto pointed toward the darkened trees. "What kind of bird makes that sound?"

"That's not a bird," laughed Angela. "That's a raccoon and from the sound of it, I think it's a momma looking for her babies."

"It is wonderful that you know these things. Growing up in Florida the only night sounds I heard were automobile horns and sirens."

Angela was quiet for a minute. Then she asked, "Do you think Monica is sorry she and Steve moved here? She seems so different than she was back in Florida."

"*Si*, she did seem unhappy but I am not sure if it is because of West Virginia or because of Mr. Walton."

"J.B.? He's not so bad. Do you think he

33

was trying to frighten us with that story?"

"Steve said the people around here are suspicious of newcomers. Maybe Mr. Walton thinks his story will scare us away. And Steve and Monica as well."

"Maybe. But I kind of like his wife."

"And you like it here. Don't you?" Gilberto patted Angela's hand.

"It feels right." She sighed.

Gilberto and Angela fell asleep in the chairs, wrapped in blankets, holding hands, listening to the gentle sounds of the night and dreaming about the future.

3
MAKING THE ROUNDS

The phone was ringing off the wall as Angela walked into Monica's kitchen. "Aren't you going to answer that?" she asked.

"No," muttered Monica. "It's a party line and that's not our ring."

"What do you mean *not your ring?*"

"Years ago when the phone company ran lines into the hollow there were too few people to make private lines economical so they put in party lines. Three or four families shared a line and their individual telephone numbers generated two, three or four rings."

"And they've never updated the system?"

"Nope."

"What if you pick up on someone else's ring?"

"Then you get to eavesdrop."

"No kidding?" Angela was fascinated by the whole idea.

"Why would I kid about something like

that?" Monica frowned.

"Doesn't all that ringing drive you crazy?"

"You have no idea." Monica reached for the coffee pot and held it out to Angela. "Want some coffee?"

"Thought you'd never ask. Gil and I were up pretty late last night sitting by the river and listening to all the animals."

"Peaceful, isn't it?" Monica stared out the window and sighed.

"I can't believe how much it reminds me of Indiana." Angela sipped her coffee.

"Hey, here's an idea," suggested Monica. "After breakfast you and I should take the Jeep and make the rounds. I'll take you into town so you can see what's there and then maybe we can swing by the old cemetery."

"What about Steve and Gil?" asked Angela.

"Oh, I'm sure Steve will find something to keep Gil busy. Speaking of which, how long do you think he's going to sleep? This is a farm, after all. We're normally *up and out at the crack of dawn.*"

Angela caught the not-so-subtle hint. "Put some bread in the toaster. I'll go wake him right now."

Following a farm-size breakfast of ham, eggs, hash browns, toast and homemade apple butter, Angela and Monica took the

Jeep and went one way while Steve and Gil jumped in the truck and went the other. Although it was pushing ten a.m. the sun hadn't made its way over the ridge yet and heavy dew covered the grass, weeds and low-lying shrubs. If it had been a couple of degrees colder there would have been frost. Angela remembered to bring a warm jacket but she'd forgotten gloves. Sticking her hands in her armpits, she asked Monica if the Jeep had a heater.

Monica chuckled. "Yes, but it doesn't work. Once we get out of the hollow, we'll be in sunlight and this thing will get so warm you'll think you're back in Florida."

Angela wondered if that was where Monica wanted to be.

The Jeep bounced wildly down the rutted road missing most of the large rocks but hitting several potholes. "You don't wear dentures, do you?" asked Monica.

"Not yet," replied Angela. "But I might need them by the time we get to town."

Monica laughed and gunned the engine. "Well, let's see how fast we can get there."

Before she could worry about her safety, Angela realized they were out of the hollow and on the hardtop road. As promised, the sun filled the sky and the temperature inside the Jeep rose to an almost tolerable level.

Looking out the window, she noticed that life on the hardtop moved at a faster pace than down in the hollows. Driving out of the hollow, she hadn't seen another living soul. Out here it seemed people were, how did Monica put it? Up and out before the crack of dawn? On one side of the road, a farmer was unloading hay for his livestock. Did he raise pigs? On the other side, an empty yellow school bus sat parked. Was it broken down or just waiting for riders to arrive? A beat-up truck with the words *Farm Use Only* painted on the doors slowly crossed the highway. Where was the driver headed and what was he going to do once he got there? Obviously, there were advantages to living on the paved road. Like not having to yield to other drivers and having a lot more sunlight. But there were disadvantages as well, such as more traffic, more noise and less privacy. If given the choice, Angela believed she would choose the hollows.

Monica blew through a yellow caution light, whipped around a corner and pulled into a grocery store parking lot.

"What?" teased Angela. "No Wal-Mart?"

"Hey, we're lucky to have this place," replied Monica. "The only other grocery store is thirty miles away. I usually only drive in once a week but I thought you'd like to see the town." She spread her arms. "This is it. Whaddaya think?"

Town consisted of four blocks surrounding a red brick building that housed the police department, jail, public services and mayor's offices, the county extension agent's office, and a small senior center. The grocery store and a hardware store took up one of the blocks, a drugstore, bank and barbershop another, a resale store and movie house the third, and a bus stop and diner the last. There didn't appear to be any bars, beauty shops or dentist offices. Maybe they were hidden away where no one would see them. Or maybe people out here didn't have a need for them.

"We'll run into the grocery and pick up some donuts," declared Monica. "I always take something when I go visiting."

"We're going visiting?" Angela wondered if the trip to town was going to be business or social.

"Yeah, there are some people I want you to meet."

While inside the store, Monica took a moment to introduce Angela to the bakery clerk. "Jasper, I want you to meet Angela Fontero." Her introduction sounded like an edict. "She and her husband are visiting from Florida."

"No kidding? I've always wanted to see Florida but it's just so fur I never made it. Is it as purty as people say?"

"Oh, yes," replied Angela. "Lots of palm trees and, of course, the ocean." She wasn't sure what else to say. Too much might be over the man's head; too little might insult his intelligence.

"I saw the ocean when me and the wife went to North Carolina last year but I never bin to Florida."

The young man was chewing on something. Was it tobacco? Angela smiled and tried to ignore his bulging cheek. "Well, I'm sure you'll make it someday."

Monica pointed toward the bakery counter. "Are the donuts fresh?"

"Yup," replied the clerk. "Jist got a delivery today. Fer the weekend. Ya know how everyone likes their sweets on the weekend."

"Yes, I do," replied Monica. "As a matter of fact, why don't you bring a box to church on Sunday? I'm sure everyone would enjoy coffee and donuts after the service."

"Not sure we're gonna make it." Jasper hung his head and shuffled his feet. "The wife's mother is coming in and she be partial to the Baptist church down in Muddville."

"Really?" Monica's eyes narrowed and her eyebrows scrunched. "Well, maybe next week?"

"Maybe." Jasper shifted his chaw from one cheek to the other but didn't look up.

Monica grabbed three boxes of donuts and pushed Angela toward the checkout. "Let's get out of here before I lose my temper." Her face was turning red.

"Why? What's wrong?" Angela wasn't sure what had just happened but whatever it was had upset Monica.

"That's the same kind of response we've been getting from people ever since we moved here," hissed Monica. "They're either too busy, too tired, or too whatever to come to our service. It's like we have the plague or something." She paid for the donuts and rushed out of the store.

"Is that what's upsetting you?" Angela ran to keep up with Monica.

"Upset? I'm not upset. What would make you think that?"

Deciding not to antagonize Monica any further, Angela climbed into the Jeep and pulled the cloth door shut. "So where to now?"

"Pawpaw," barked Monica. "It's a small town about five miles up the road. No stores or anything — just a few old houses. A

41

woman named Gelah lives there."

Now that Angela knew what was bothering Monica she understood why she seemed so agitated. She'd given up her palatial triple wide trailer in Florida for a rundown old house in the middle of nowhere, left all her loving friends for people who didn't trust her, and her Jeep didn't have a heater. Could things get any worse?

The ride to Pawpaw passed in awkward silence. When Monica finally pulled up in front of a small, buttercup-yellow house, she grabbed a box of donuts and ordered, "Let's go." Angela trailed two steps behind.

The inside of Gelah Spears' house looked like a museum. Lace doilies protected the backs, arms, and tops of what appeared to be antique furniture. Sepia-toned framed photos lined the walls. A well-used family Bible sat open on a black wrought iron stand.

Monica made quick introductions. "Gelah, I'd like you to meet Angela Fontero. Angela, this is Gelah Spears."

Gelah's white hair was pulled back and twisted neatly into a bun at the nape of her neck. She wore a simple cotton housedress cinched by a floral apron and she smelled of talcum powder and soap. Angela immediately liked her.

"I love your doilies," remarked Angela. "Did you make them yourself?"

"Why, yes I did," replied Gelah. "But they're not doilies, they're antimacassars."

"Anti what?" Angela wondered if she'd heard correctly.

"During the early 1800s people used Makassar oil to groom their hair. Unfortunately, the oil left stains whenever someone sat down and rested their head against the sofa. In order to minimize the stains, women started crocheting antimacassars and placing them on the backs of chairs, sofas and fainting couches, making it possible for their guests to rest their heads without leaving stains." Gelah sat on the sofa, patted the cushions, and invited Angela and Monica to join her.

"That's fascinating." Angela wasn't sure if she was more impressed with the doilies or the fact that the woman was so educated. "Where did you learn to make them?"

"My mother taught me, her mother taught her, and so on. Guess you could say the art has been in my family for more than two hundred years."

"How long have you lived in Pawpaw?" asked Angela.

"Just since I got married," replied Gelah. "I was born in Stringtown but that house is long gone. My husband was a traveling salesman — we called them drummers back then. He built this house in 1953 and I've been here ever since."

"Tell Angela about your children, Gelah," suggested Monica.

"Well . . . I raised six of my own, Matthew, Luke, Elizabeth, Mark, John, and Mary. When they grew up and moved away I took in about twenty foster kids."

Angela gasped. "Twenty? At one time?"

"Gracious, no. Just four or five at a time."

"And they all lived in this house?"

"Yes. There are three bedrooms in the back and a loft in the attic."

"How many live here now?" asked Angela.

"Oh, they're all gone. Now it's just me."

"Don't you get lonely?"

"Heavens no. I have my memories and my Bible. What more could anyone want?"

Monica leaned toward Gelah. "Speaking of Bibles, how about coming to church this Sunday? Steve or I could come pick you up. Or maybe even Angela and her new husband. You'd like that, wouldn't you?"

"You have a new husband?" Gelah took Angela's hand in hers. "What's his name?"

"Gilberto." Angela felt her face blush. "He's Italian."

"Can he cook?" The old woman's eyes

twinkled.

"He used to be a chef in one of Florida's largest hotels," laughed Angela.

"I'd like to meet him."

"That settles it." Monica grabbed Angela's arm and pulled her toward the door. "We'll pick you up Sunday morning at nine."

"Can't you stay a while longer?" begged Gelah.

"We'd love to," replied Monica. "But I promised to show Angela around some more. We'll have more time to visit on Sunday. See you then." She was out the door before Gelah could stop her.

"It was lovely seeing you." Gelah waved as Monica and Angela quickly drove away.

"Why did we have to leave so fast?" asked Angela. "She seemed like such a nice lady. I would have liked to talk to her some more."

"I've been trying to get her to come to church for three months. This was the first time she said yes. There was no way I was going to let her change her mind."

Angela knew Steve and Monica were trying to get people interested in their church but the way Monica had just acted bordered on desperation. What if they couldn't build a congregation? Would they pack up and move back to Florida? Knowing Steve, the answer would be *No*. Knowing Monica, he'd probably be overruled.

Before long, the Jeep was climbing a steep hill. At the top was an old house and just below it, a long-neglected cemetery.

"This is Hummingbird Ridge," announced Monica. "If you look down below the cemetery, you'll see our farm."

"Wow," exclaimed Angela. "I didn't realize we'd come that far."

"When you take the road through the hollow, you wind around a lot. This ridge joins the hardtop and then it's a short ride down to the farm."

"Straight down?" Based on Monica's performance driving out of the hollow, Angela wasn't all that sure she wanted to chance a downhill slalom. At least not with Monica at the wheel.

"What's the matter? Heights make you nervous?"

Angela swallowed hard and followed as Monica led the way to the cemetery.

"As far as we can tell, this cemetery was here before our farm. Some of the tombstones are so old the dates are worn off."

"Is this the cemetery J.B. mentioned?"

"Yes, but I'm sure we're not going to see Mr. and Mrs. Withers."

"Really? I was sort of looking forward to it." Angela laughed and walked around the tombstones. "Which ones are theirs?"

"I don't know," snapped Monica. "I never really looked for them."

"Are we still on your property?" asked Angela.

"Yes. But we don't own the cemetery. Our deed specifically excludes it."

"What about that house?" Angela pointed toward the top of the ridge. Although weathered and surrounded by weeds, the house looked sturdy. None of the windows was broken, the roof seemed intact and its two stories were bathed in sunlight.

"That old thing? Yeah, it's on our property. But who cares? We'll probably tear it down as soon as we get a chance."

"Why?" asked Angela.

"It's an eyesore and it's probably filled with black snakes and field mice."

"Can we go in?"

"What for?"

"I love old houses. I'd like to see what's inside." Angela started walking toward the house.

"I don't think that's a good idea." Monica tried to grab Angela's arm but she wasn't fast enough.

"Come on, Monica. Where's your spirit of adventure?" She raced toward the house.

"Oh, all right. But the first snake I see,

I'm outta there."

When she reached the steps, Angela cautioned Monica. "Watch that middle one, I nearly put my foot through it."

"Thanks for telling me." Monica muttered something as she pulled her shoe out of the rotted step.

Except for a few broken chairs, the inside of the house was barren. There were no obvious snakes but tiny footprints in the dust indicated mice were frequent visitors. Angela ran up the stairs. "Monica, come look."

The second floor was divided into two large bedrooms. In one, there was an old brass headboard; in the other, a baby's crib. The two women walked into the second room and placed their hands on the crib.

"Are you sorry you never had kids?" asked Monica.

Angela walked to the window. It stretched almost the full length between the ceiling and floor. A single curtain rod was nailed to the framework but the curtain was long gone. She rubbed the dirt away from one of the panes. "I had one before I got married — a girl. But my parents insisted I give her up." The minute the words were out of her mouth, she wanted to draw them back. But it was too late.

"Why would they do that?" Monica had no way of knowing how sensitive Angela was about the subject.

"It was before being a single mother was fashionable."

"Yeah, but couldn't they have raised her for you?"

Angela flicked a dead wasp from the window sash to the floor. "They didn't want to. They said they had already raised all the children they wanted and they didn't need to start over again. But it was all right, she went to a good home."

"Did you ever try to see her?"

"No. I didn't think I had a right to interfere in her life."

Angela wished she hadn't confided in Monica. It wasn't as if they were friends. Not like her and Katherine, anyway. Katherine had cried when Angela told her about her daughter. Where were Monica's tears?

"Does Gil know?" probed Monica.

"Yes. I told him." Monica was asking way too many questions. Looking for a way to change the subject, Angela was relieved when she spotted a truck driving up the road toward Monica's farm. "Hey, isn't that the guys?"

Monica looked out the window. "Yes, it is. Looks like they're finished with whatever they were doing. How about you? Wanna go back or keep exploring?"

"If you don't mind, I'd like to go back into town to see if I can find a souvenir for Gil." Angela prayed Monica would forget about their conversation. If not, she'd just have to find a way to deal with it.

"Sure, but we'll have to start back by two. I think Steve's got something planned for dinner and I might need to supervise."

After walking through every store in town and finding absolutely nothing, Angela and Monica headed back to the farm. When they arrived, they found Steve and Gil in the kitchen, pots boiling on the stove, and a bunch of empty cans littering the table.

Monica crossed her arms. "I'm gone a couple of hours and you destroy my kitchen?"

Steve pointed his finger at Gilberto. "Blame it on him. He ransacked the cabinets and said we had everything he needed for a perfect dinner."

"Oh yeah?" questioned Monica. "What's he making?"

"It is a surprise," announced Gilberto. "But I am sure you will like it."

Angela and Monica were ushered out to wait on the front porch while the men completed their preparations. When they were finally called into the house, the dining room table was set, the candles were lit and both men were wearing suits.

Angela looked impressed. "The only things missing are roses and violins."

Gilberto produced two silk roses while Steve inserted a cassette into a boom box.

Steve bowed. "Ladies, may we seat you?" Gilberto uncovered the serving dishes.

"Spaghetti?" gasped Monica. "You call that the perfect dinner?"

"*Sì,* in my country, it is perfecto." Gilberto acted offended.

Dinner was wonderful. The pasta was *al dente,* the sauce was *molto buono* and the service was *magnifico.* Between mouthfuls, Angela told Gilberto about her day with Monica. "We checked out all the stores in town and I met a lady named Gelah who's coming to church on Sunday."

Steve cheered. "How'd you do that?"

"I promised to introduce her to Gil."

"Way to go. Maybe I should keep you around."

Angela giggled and wiped some fugitive spaghetti sauce from her chin. "We also went through a great old house up by the cemetery."

"You must mean the old Sergeant place," said Steve. "From what I hear, Sergeant sort of took care of the cemetery. I don't know whatever happened to him but I've been in that house. It's not bad."

Angela didn't try to hide her enthusiasm. "It sits right on top of the ridge where it's nice and sunny so all the rooms were filled with light. There's a huge country kitchen and a living room with a fireplace downstairs and two good-sized bedrooms upstairs. With a little bit of paint and elbow grease, it would make a really nice home."

"What about plumbing? Was there a bathroom?" Gilberto seemed to know where Angela's chain of thought was leading.

"From what I could see, there was just an outhouse."

"I am sure a bathroom could be added if someone wanted to go through all the trouble." A knowing grin spread across Gilberto's face.

Angela laid down her fork and stared into her husband's eyes. "Are you thinking what I'm thinking?"

4
COUNTRY WAYS

Three months after their wedding, Angela and Gil moved to Hummingbird Ridge. Steve had the electricity turned on and got a couple of neighbors to install a makeshift bathroom in the old house, but not much of anything else was changed. The stairs were still rotted, some of the warped doors wouldn't close and dust-covered cobwebs hung from every corner.

Gizmo seemed to love his new surroundings. He sniffed his way around as if he'd been born there, chased groundhogs and land turtles, and even caught his first mouse which Angela named Mickey before setting it adrift down the new toilet. Gil suggested putting up a fence so the dog wouldn't get into trouble but Angela pooh-poohed the idea saying it sounded too much like jail.

While waiting for their furniture to arrive, the newlyweds spent most of their time working on the house. But by the eighth day, they were running out of things to do so Angela decided to repaint all the windows. Maintaining the farmhouse character, she chose white, the same color the previous owners used. It would go with anything and, if she missed a spot, it wouldn't show. When she had trouble opening the kitchen window, she asked Gil for help. After a quick examination, he determined the window had been painted shut.

Angela frowned. "Why would anyone do that?"

"Most likely to keep the weather out."

"You mean like insulation?"

"*Sí*. Insulation."

"Well, that's just plain silly. What if they wanted fresh air?"

Gilberto shrugged his shoulders and grinned. "Maybe they went outside."

As Gilberto and Angela struggled to free the window, they heard Steve's truck screech to a halt in front of the house. Steve stuck his head out the truck window and yelled, "Come quick. There's been an accident down the road."

Angela and Gilberto slid into the seat behind Monica. "Was anyone hurt?"

"No," replied Steve. "But I don't think you're gonna be happy when you see what's happened."

Steve turned the truck around and sped down the hill. It dawned on Angela that she didn't feel any safer than if Monica had been driving. She closed her eyes and braced one hand on the front seat and the other on Gilberto's knee. When they reached the paved road, she tightened her hold as they raced toward the accident.

"Where are we going?" Gilberto squirmed under Angela's death-grip.

"Up ahead," shouted Steve.

Within seconds, they came upon several cars and trucks parked in the middle of the road. From below the embankment, they heard men yelling. And then they saw it — the moving truck.

Steve and Gilberto jumped out of the truck and ran ahead as Monica and Angela picked their way through weeds and rocks.

"Watch for snakes," cautioned Monica.

"Yeah, I know." Angela was beginning to think Monica was paranoid.

The truck was flipped over with all of its wheels pointed toward the sky. The disoriented driver stood next to it scratching his head.

"That's not *our* moving truck, is it?" Angela forgot about snakes and ran to join Gilberto.

"I'm afraid so," replied Steve.

"How did this happen?" asked Gilberto.

"The driver thought he could get to Hummingbird Ridge off this road but he didn't know where the turnoff was. So when he saw the mail carrier coming from the opposite direction he pulled over to ask directions. I guess the weight of the loaded van was too much and the road collapsed sending the truck rolling toward the river. If it had rolled one more time it would have been in the water."

"Was the driver in the truck when it started to roll?" Angela's face showed her concern.

"No. He and the mailman were standing in the road when it happened."

"Thank goodness." Relieved that no one was hurt, Angela and Gilberto walked toward the truck. The rear door had sprung open and boxes were scattered along the riverbank. Inside, chairs and tables were heaped in a twisted mess.

"What will happen now?" asked Gilberto.

"The driver called his dispatcher and they're going to send out a wrecker. But that won't happen until tomorrow or the next day so I guess you'll have to spend a couple more nights in the trailer." Steve sounded apologetic.

"Maybe not." Digging through the boxes,

Angela looked like a kid opening birthday presents. "Look. I just found our blankets and pillows. We can pretend we're camping and cuddle up in front of the fireplace. How's that for romantic?"

Gilberto smiled and hugged his wife.

Steve and Monica helped load some of the other boxes into their truck. On the way back to Hummingbird Ridge, Monica offered to cook Sunday dinner. "It's Easter and you shouldn't have to spend it in an empty house. Steve is baking a country ham and I'm making my world-famous potato salad."

"I love your potato salad," squealed Angela. "Hey, do you know if anyone around here grows horseradish? My mom used to make the best homemade horseradish sauce. It would go great with the ham."

"I don't know," replied Monica. "Ask Pam. Maybe she'd know."

"Good idea."

Later that afternoon, Angela walked down the road toward the Walton farm. Under normal circumstances, she would have called before popping in on anyone but since she didn't have a phone yet, she had no other choice. Even so, she worried. Based on some of the things Monica said, J.B.'s wife might not be all that happy to see her. What if she ran her off? Or worse, what if she met her at the door with a shotgun? Maybe this wasn't such a good idea after all. When she finally reached the house, she knocked on the door, stood back, and hoped Pam's response would at least be cordial.

"Well, I'll be," exclaimed Pam. "Thought you'd still be up at the river. Is something wrong?"

"Oh, no, nothing is wrong," replied Angela. "I just came by to ask if you knew if anyone in the hollow grew horseradish."

"Sure. What do you want it for?"

"Steve is making ham for Sunday and I thought I'd whip up some fresh horseradish sauce."

"Have you ever made it before?"

"No, but I watched my mom."

"Well come on in and set a spell. We can have coffee then I'll take you out back and we'll dig up some nice roots."

Pam's living room floor was covered with floral linoleum that had seen its share of scrubbings, boots and dog claws. Off to one side were two bedrooms and a bath. Up ahead was the kitchen. Pam filled a kettle with water and placed a jar of instant coffee on the table. "I have tea if you'd rather." She ran her fingers through her hair then rubbed her hands on the back of her jeans.

"Coffee will be fine." Angela noticed a faded print of the Last Supper on the wall behind the table. There had been a cross on the living room wall when she first walked in. Obviously, these people were religious. So why was J.B. so dead set against Steve and Monica?

When the kettle whistled, Pam poured water into two bowl-sized mugs. Angela frowned as she spooned instant coffee into hers. The water was a strange orange color.

"That's well water," said Pam. "There's a lot of iron in it. That's what gives it the color. And the smell."

Angela raised the mug to her nose. It smelled like rotten eggs.

"Don't worry. It won't hurt you," assured Pam. "The County tested it last year and said it was safe to drink."

Angela stirred the coffee and took a sip. "Do you have any milk or cream?"

Pam laughed and pulled a jar of powdered whitener from the cabinet. "Here. Will this do?"

The two women talked and drank coffee for about an hour before Angela's curiosity got the better of her. "Why won't J.B. go to Steve's church?"

"J.B. doesn't like preachers that weren't

raised in the hollows. Says they're all do-gooders who say we have to change our ways or we'll burn in hell. Says they don't care about our ways, just their own."

"Steve isn't trying to change anyone, he's only trying to help."

"Doesn't make a difference. J.B. is set in his ways. He doesn't take to newcomers telling him what to do. Or anyone in his family, either." Pam rose from her chair and headed for the back door. "Now, let's get that horseradish. J.B. and the boys will be wanting their supper soon."

Angela wanted to ask Pam why it was okay for J.B. to eat dinner at the new preacher's house but not okay for him to attend his church. She didn't get a chance. Pam marched out the door and led the way to the back of the garden where several long-leafed green plants grew.

Wielding a rusted garden fork, Pam loosened, then yanked two long roots from the ground. After brushing the dirt and worms free, she handed them to Angela. "This should be enough for your dinner." Her tone had turned cool. "Make sure you wash them well before you grind them. No one likes anything foreign in their horseradish."

Or in their hollow, thought Angela.

She thanked Pam for the horseradish,

returned home and started digging through the salvaged boxes. Realizing she had never owned a traditional hand grater, she opted for a food blender. "After all," she muttered, "it has a grater button."

After washing, peeling and chopping the roots, she placed a handful in the blender, added a little vinegar and salt and pressed the grater button. The machine bounced and twirled across the countertop but eventually settled down and turned the lanky root into a lily-white gruel. Wondering if it smelled anything like her mother's, she removed the top of the blender and took a big sniff. All at once, her sinuses swelled up, her eyelids clamped shut and her lungs refused to take in air. Fifteen minutes later, Gilberto found her sitting on the floor, cradling her head in both hands and sobbing.

"What has happened, *amore mio?*" Gilberto knelt on the floor beside his wife.

Angela raised her head. Her nose was running, her eyes were tearing and she was starting to get the worst headache she had ever experienced. Even so, she managed to squeeze out a pathetic, "I made horseradish."

The following Sunday, everyone had something to say about the horseradish.

"You should have known the heat from that blender would create toxic fumes." Monica used her *nun* voice.

Steve laughed. "Hindsight is everything. I'll bet you never do that again."

"Be nice," scolded Gelah. She and two neighbors had attended Steve's Easter service. Monica invited all three of them to dinner but Gelah was the only one to accept. "Country life takes a lot of getting used to."

"My wife is eager to learn everything she can." Gilberto squeezed Angela's hand. "I am also eager because everything here is so different from Florida."

Gelah nodded and smiled. "Well, I've been around for a long time. I'll tell you anything you want to know."

"Do you have any special Easter traditions or customs?" asked Steve.

"No, not really. Like everyone else, I always hid colored eggs for the children and told that old legend about the dogwoods."

"What are dogwoods?" asked Gilberto. "I do not believe we had them in Florida."

"Dogwoods are twisted little mountain shrubs that flower every year around Easter," replied Gelah. "Their blossoms can be either white or pink but they're always tinged with tiny red drops."

"Always?" asked Angela.

"Well, not always." Gelah smiled and took a deep breath. "You see, a long time ago, the dogwood was a tall, straight tree. People favored its wood for furniture, barns and even houses. One day, a carpenter was asked to build a very large cross. Now the carpenter wondered why anyone needed such a big cross but he didn't ask any questions because he had a big family to feed and needed the money."

"How long ago was this?" asked Gilberto.

"A good long time ago," replied Gelah. "So the man goes into the woods, finds a great big tree, chops it down and drags it home. Next day he starts to work. It took two days but when he was finished he stood back and admired his work. He had done such a good job he was sure people would ask him to build many other things."

Steve nodded as if he'd heard the story before.

"Early the next morning the carpenter loaded the cross onto a cart and took it to the town market. When some soldiers saw him, they started yelling. 'You fool. Don't you know you were supposed to take that cross to the jail? They're crucifying a criminal today and they want him to drag his cross up the hill. If you don't hurry up, we'll nail you up instead.'

"The carpenter didn't want to get into any trouble so he did as he was told and took the cross to the jail where another soldier gave him a couple coins for his work. Then, not knowing what else to do, he decided to stay and see what was going to happen next.

"A tall man with long dark hair and a dark beard was dragged out of the jail. On his head was a ring of thorns and over his shoulders was a dirty red cape. One of the soldiers ripped the cape off the man's shoulders and ordered him to carry the cross. The carpenter was frightened so he stayed at the back of the crowd. He watched as the tall man stumbled through the streets, he watched as he fell and he watched as a woman ran up to him and wiped the blood away from his face."

Everyone's eyes were glued on Gelah.

"When the man got to the top of a hill, some soldiers nailed him to the cross. The sky grew dark and lightning filled the air. The carpenter made his way through the crowd and stood at the foot of the cross as the man died. Then he knelt down and begged God's forgiveness." Gelah lowered her head and sighed before finishing her story.

"No one knows whatever became of that

carpenter but ever since that day, dogwoods have never grown into tall trees. At least not in these parts. Their trunks are thin and twisted and they have blossoms that have four petals in the shape of the cross. The outer edge of each petal shows tiny nail prints tinged with red and the center looks like a crown of thorns."

"Wow," exclaimed Angela. "What a wonderful story. Is it true?"

"My parents told me that story when I was a little girl and over the years, I told it to all my children. Even my grans. I've never questioned it. Some things, you just have to accept on face value."

"Why do all the people out here insist on telling such far-fetched stories?" Monica didn't seem impressed with the story.

Gelah refolded the napkin on her lap and looked Monica in the eye. "Well, you see, living in these hollows, a lot of us didn't have much opportunity for schooling and for a long time we didn't even have radios or television. Our parents told stories to educate and entertain us and we told those same stories to our children."

"Sort of like urban legends?" asked Steve.

"Yes, but we like to call them folk tales."

"What's the difference?"

Gelah smiled. "Most urban legends are

65

nothing more than elaborate hoaxes or unsubstantiated myths. Folk tales are all about history, morals, values and traditions."

"Sounds the same to me," mumbled Monica.

"Not really," replied Gelah. "If you forget an urban legend, you have lost nothing. Anyone can make up a new one. If you forget your stories, you lose who you are. It's sort of like trust. Once you lose it, you never get it back."

Angela leaned back and looked around the room. Everyone sitting at that table had a story of their own. She had grown up in a small farm-town in Indiana; Gil came from Italy and lived an affluent life in Florida; Steve and Monica had been missionaries in war-torn Nicaragua; and Gelah had raised her kids and lived her entire life in the hollows of West Virginia. They seemed so different, yet they seemed so alike. All of them were intelligent; all of them had lived through rough times, all of them believed in God. There had to be a way they could forget their differences or at least learn to accept them.

But how?

5
WOMEN'S WORK

The first thing Angela did after her phone was installed was call her friend, Katherine. Even though it had only been a couple of weeks since they'd talked, it seemed like years. Angela missed Katherine and her carefree attitude about everything. It was as if life was one great big party and she didn't want to miss a minute of it. *Could that sort of thing rub off?*

Katherine giggled when she heard Angela's voice. "Sooo . . . how's country life treating you? You and Gil been for a roll in the hay yet?"

"No, but it sounds like fun. Wish we had a barn." Angela giggled but kept right on talking. "I love it here," she proclaimed. "The air is clean, there are no alligators or hurricanes and it's so quiet you can hear your heart beat."

"Or your arteries hardening."

"No, really, it's wonderful. Everything is

so different."

"Yeah? Like what?"

"Well, for one thing, we're talking on a party line."

"What's that?" Katherine's voice jumped two full notches.

"We share the phone line with three other families in the hollow." Actually, it was only two but three sounded more rural.

"You mean someone could be listening in?"

There was a loud click and both women started laughing. Gulping air, Angela barely managed to reply, "Not anymore."

Katherine brayed like a donkey. "Okay, so what else?"

"Well, last week Gil went into town and bought his first pair of blue jeans."

"Whoopee." Katherine didn't sound impressed.

"When he got home, he put them on and suggested we go for a walk."

"Why? Did he want to show off to the chipmunks?"

"We don't have chipmunks here. The raccoons ate them all."

"Eeew."

Angela pictured Katherine's expression and laughed. "Anyway, we were walking through one of our neighbor's cornfields when Gil started to complain about something rubbing."

"What'd he do? Forget to remove the price tag?"

"No. The denim was so stiff it was rubbing against his leg. He sat down in the middle of the field, took the jeans off and discovered a great big red splotch."

"Where?"

"Don't ask."

Katherine snickered. "Oh no. Then what?"

"I told him to take his shirt off and wrap it around his waist so he'd be covered up while we walked back home."

"That must have been attractive."

"In a strange sort of a way, it was. I don't know what came over me but when he took his shirt off and I saw his farmer's tan, I guess I got kind of carried away. And, well, one thing led to another . . ."

"You didn't." Katherine shrieked into the phone.

"We did. Right there in front of God and all those marvelous hay stalks."

"Did anyone see you?"

"Not that I know of."

"I can see it now. Farmer Brown goes out on his tractor and comes upon two lovebirds building a nest smack dab in the middle of his field. He tries to look away but notices the lovebirds are old enough to be his grandparents. Not knowing whether to call the cops or the rescue squad, he just stands there and gawks."

"More likely he runs home, tells his wife and she gets on the phone and tells all the neighbors."

"Would that happen?" asked Katherine.

"Oh yeah," chuckled Angela.

"Charming. So what other fun things have you been doing?"

"Gizmo caught a mouse, I made home-made horseradish and Monica is upset because no one goes to Steve's church."

"No one?" Katherine sounded shocked.

"Well, practically no one. There's this wonderful lady named Gelah that always comes and she usually brings a couple of friends with her. But no one from the hollow has attended any of the services. Not even on Easter Sunday."

"What's the problem?" questioned Katherine.

"Steve thinks it's because no one really knows him yet but one of the neighbors said it's because he and Monica are newcomers who just want to change everything to suit themselves."

"That's ridiculous. They were missionaries in Nicaragua. They're all about helping

70

people, not changing them."

"I know," replied Angela. "But things are different here."

"In what way?"

"Well, in Nicaragua the people wanted Steve and Monica's help." Her voice trembled as she finished the thought. "Out here, they'd just as soon not have it."

"Does that bother you?" asked Katherine.

"Well, sure it does. Steve and Monica gave us this house. We didn't have to buy the land and they're not even charging us rent. They treat us like family. I guess I feel we owe them."

"You're kidding, right?" Disbelief laced Katherine's tone.

"No. I'm not. You may not know this but for the first time in my life, I have a home I can call my own. As a kid, I lived in my parents' house. When I got married, the farm was in Carl's name. Once I was out on my own, I moved from rental to rental. Even the trailer in Florida belonged to someone else. I never felt like I really belonged anywhere." She took a deep breath, as much for effect as necessity. "Here in West Virginia, my life has changed. I have a wonderful husband who treats me like a queen. I wake up every morning to the sound of my neighbor's rooster crowing at sunrise. The forest animals make me smile and the trees and the mountains give me strength. I feel alive, as if I could do great things even though I don't know what those things are. This is the place I want to be . . . the place I want to stay. I know it's probably being selfish but Gil and I are just starting our life together. We want to see Steve make a go of his church and we want to be a part of making that happen."

"Wow, that's pretty heavy. So what are you gonna do?" asked Katherine.

"Me? What can I do?"

"I don't know. Maybe something that would convince everyone that Steve isn't trying to change their world."

"That's easier said than done. The women in this hollow are old-fashioned. The men are practically primordial."

"So, start with the women," suggested Katherine.

"How?"

"You could get them involved in some kind of club like I did in Florida."

"You mean the Foxy Ladies?" Angela's mind drifted as Katherine continued to babble. Even though it sounded a little far-fetched, she realized her redheaded friend's suggestion held some merit. Aside from watching soap operas and gossiping on the party line, there wasn't much the women in the hollow could do once their chores were done. Some sort of club might interest them. They could get together, share ideas and maybe have a little fun. But the Foxy Ladies? That was a bit of a stretch. Even if some of the women wanted to go out for lunch once in a while, they probably didn't have enough money to spend on something so frivolous. No, the Foxy Ladies was totally out of the question. But what about starting a sewing circle or arts and crafts group? Maybe even a cooking club or recipe exchange. Something that would fit into the women's country lives. But what did she know about starting a club? She'd spent most of her adult life working in a hardware store. When she wasn't working, she was sleeping, cleaning house or rescuing stray dogs. There had been very little time for joining clubs or socializing.

Katherine's shrill voice broke through Angela's concentration. "Hey, where'd you go? Are you even listening to me?"

"I'm sorry," apologized Angela. "I was thinking about what you said and maybe you were right." Then, even knowing she might be biting off more than she could chew, she asked the important question: "What do I do first?"

Katherine jumped at the opportunity to give advice. "Call one of your neighbor ladies and say you need help sewing curtains or something. Tell her you've never been good with a needle and that you'd be *forever* indebted if she and a couple of her friends gave you a hand. You could even suggest everyone bring something for a potluck lunch. Of course, you'd have to meet at the church because that's where the windows are. But tell them Steve and Monica won't be there so it wouldn't be as if they were going to church or anything. Get the women used to the place and before long they'll be dragging their husbands along."

"Think it will work?"

"You'll never know unless you try."

Angela went to work. Over the next couple of days, she called Pam and Sharon, bought ten yards of gingham, scrubbed the church floor and baked a chocolate cake. Both excited and nervous, she found it hard to concentrate on anything else. One night, she totally forgot about making dinner and she and Gil ended up eating beans and franks. He didn't complain, of course, but Angela knew he was still hungry when he raided the refrigerator an hour later and made himself a peanut butter and jelly sandwich.

The following Saturday, Angela's heart sank when Pam showed up at the church alone. Trying to hide her disappointment, she began to wonder what to do next. Should she send Pam home? Act like nothing was wrong? Hide under a pew? When Sharon and her two daughters walked in five minutes later, she felt almost giddy.

"I weren't too sure about coming," said Sharon. "My husband toll me it went aginst our ways. Said God was gonna strike me dead. Well, here I am and I ain't dead yet, so I guess he were wrong. She took one look at the fabric and immediately disapproved. "You cain't put gingham curtains in'a church. It jist ain't right. They's gotta be lace or sumppin white. You know — like pure. Kathy Sue? Run home right quick and get those ol' tablecloths I bin keeping in the attic. We'll make us some proper curtains for this here church."

The work went fast. Pam and Angela cut the fabric while Sharon and her daughters did the sewing. Forgetting there was no electricity in the church, the sewing machine Angela brought along was useless. But it didn't matter because the girls' hand stitching was fine and almost invisible, like what you might see in a fancy bridal shop. One by one, as each panel was finished, it was hung on a window. Within three hours, the church was transformed from a rundown old building to a charming country church.

Angela stood back and admired the curtains. "They're so beautiful. I could never have done this myself. Thank you so much."

Sharon's youngest daughter had been sucking a needle-pricked finger. Taking it out of her mouth, she asked, "Kin we eat now?" Her mother responded with a sharp swat to the back of the girl's head and a curt, "Mind yur tongue young'un."

"She's right," objected Pam. "If the men were here, the food would be gone by now." Pam headed for a sideboard where the food had been placed and started taking lids off all the dishes. Angela joined her and handed out paper plates and utensils. Once their plates were full, the women sat cross-legged on the floor and began to eat.

"This is fun," squealed Sharon. "Sort of reminds me of eatin' lunch at that old schoolhouse we used to go to. Remember that place, Pam?"

"How can I forget?" Pam stuck a finger in her mouth and worked a piece of macaroni free from her back teeth. "It was one of the oldest and draftiest buildings in Stringtown."

"That's the ghost town, right?" Angela

wanted to learn as much as she could about the hollow. Maybe that would help her understand the people who lived there.

"Yes," replied Pam. "West Virginia's always had a lot of trees and back in my great-grammas' day someone decided to start cutting them down for money. For a while they just cut trees that were easy to get to but once those were gone, they started cutting the ones in the hollows."

Angela's brow puckered like a dried-up peach. "All the way back here?"

"Sure, all the really big trees grew up on the ridges where they got lots of rain and sunshine. But the only way to get to the trees on the ridges was to go through the hollows. There weren't any real roads back then and it took the workers a long time to get into the hollows, so the logging companies put up tents so the men could stay for three or four weeks at a time. The men in this hollow called their camp Stringtown because of all the string they used to hold the tents down. Seems to me a better name would have been Ropetown. But what do I know? I'm just a woman. Anyway, when all the loggers started complaining about being away from their families, the company built houses. Of course, once they built the houses, they had to build stores, schools, post offices and churches. Just like this one. Somewhere along the way they even built a big hotel complete with a fancy dining room and saloon."

"That's amazing. But, without roads, how'd they get the trees out?"

"They floated them down the river."

"You're kidding."

Pam frowned. "Why would I kid about that? See, the logging company had sawmills set up downstream, and once those trees floated down, they were stripped, cut and loaded on to railcars that took them to market."

"Sounds like a good business. What went wrong?"

"When the Depression hit, a lot of logging companies went under. Sawmills shut down and railroad tracks were ripped out."

"What about all the families living in the logging camps?"

"Some stayed, some didn't."

"How did they support themselves?"

"The usual. They hunted, planted crops, raised kids and animals and, of course, they bartered."

"Bartered? You mean like traded?"

"Sure. No one had any money, so if someone wanted something someone else had, he traded something he had so he could get what he wanted. Both sides got something out of the deal and everyone went home happy."

"Interesting." An idea was growing in Angela's mind — one that might solve Steve and Monica's problem. "Do people in the hollow still barter?"

"All the time. Why, is there something you want?"

"Well, I was just thinking. The outside of this church could use a coat of paint. If you wouldn't mind giving me a hand, I'd get my husband to teach you some of his favorite recipes. You know — we could barter."

Sharon giggled. "Hey, that's right. He's I-Tal-E-An, ain't he? Always wanted ta learn me some fancy cookin'. Does he know how ta make pizza?"

Pam raised herself from the floor and started walking in circles. She looked like she was working on an idea of her own. "We'd need some tall ladders." She scratched her head. "J.B.'s got a couple out behind our barn. Maybe my sons could bring them."

"Well, if you think J.B. wouldn't mind, that would be great."

"They're *my* ladders, too. If he has a problem, he can take it up with me."

Angela smirked at the thought of Pam taking on her husband. He had to be a good six inches taller and fifty pounds heavier than her. But somehow, even with the odds stacked against her, Angela knew Pam would come out the winner. "Okay then. I'll go into town next week and buy some paint and brushes. We could meet back here next Saturday. Or is that too soon?"

Pam looked down at her feet and squashed an imaginary bug. "Saturday will be fine. And you might ask that preacher to give us a hand if he's a mind to."

6
SEEDS

Steve was rototilling the garden when Angela came running down the hill.

"Watch your step," he cautioned. "I spotted a snake over there a few minutes ago."

"Where?" Angela stopped dead in her tracks and refused to move. Wild mustard was coming into bloom and the hillside beneath her feet was covered in a blanket of vibrant yellow blooms.

Turning the tiller off, Steve walked toward the far corner of the garden. "Over here. You're not afraid of snakes, are you?"

"Terrified would be more accurate." Pulling up her jean legs, Angela tiptoed behind Steve. Whether it was her new lifestyle or the change of climate, her hair was growing so that now a silver-streaked mane trailed halfway down her back. It bounced from side to side as she walked. "When Carl and I had our farm in Indiana I found a snake crawling over the fence. I was afraid it would get into the house so I got my air pistol and shot it."

"Did you kill it?" asked Steve.

"Yes, but fifteen minutes later its buddy came looking for it."

Steve laughed and kicked at the loosened soil. "Well, don't worry. Most of the snakes around here are black snakes. They're not poisonous and they eat mice so they're good guys. Besides, it looks like this one is long gone."

"Thank goodness." Angela let go of her jeans, rested her hands on her hips and surveyed Steve's work. "So what are you going to plant?"

"The usual — corn, beans, tomatoes and, if I can find seeds, some hot peppers." Little sweat pearls trickled down Steve's deeply tanned face and disappeared beneath his shirt collar.

"What? No potatoes?" Ever since moving to the farm, Angela started viewing Steve more as a brother than an attractive man. It felt reassuring and made living close to him and Monica much easier.

Steve leaned into the tiller handle. "The man down at the co-op said potatoes need a lot of room so I'm going to dig up an acre on the other side of the house and plant them there. The only thing is I have to wait until the dark of the moon. He said if I planted them at any other time the roots wouldn't go deep enough and the potatoes would be small."

"Ah, yes. Planting by the moon. I remember it well. 'Roots and bulbs should be planted when the moon is waning; leafy, flowering and fruiting plants that grow above ground when it's waxing.' "

Angela took a deep breath, threw back her shoulders and gazed towards the sky. "Sure is pretty here, isn't it?" It had rained earlier in the day but now the sun broke through the wispy clouds and warmed the newly turned soil. The heady scent of dried leaves, fresh loam and earthworms drifted on the air.

"Yup, sure is," replied Steve. "Hey, listen to us. We're beginning to sound like locals. Which reminds me . . . how'd your get-together go?"

"Great. We finished all the curtains ate a nice lunch and talked about the early days of the hollow."

"Well, good. Did you enjoy yourself?"

"I did. But here's the best part." Even though she couldn't wait to blurt out the big surprise, Angela decided dragging it out would be more fun. Maybe she'd get one of Steve's gorgeous smiles as a reward. "Pam told me about how people used to barter for things and I asked if she and some of her friends would help paint the church in exchange for cooking lessons."

"*You're* going to give cooking lessons?" Steve's agate blue eyes twinkled as he spoke.

Angela jabbed his shoulder. "No, silly. Gil will give the lessons, I'll watch."

"Oh, now *that* makes more sense."

Crossing her arms, Angela raised her chin and narrowed her eyes. "Just for that, I'm not going to tell you the rest."

"There's more?"

"Yes, smarty, there's more." She turned her back and started walking toward the house. "Maybe Monica will be more interested than you."

"All right, I'm sorry. Tell me the rest."

Angela stopped walking but didn't turn around. "Whaddaya say?"

"Please?" he begged.

She took a few more steps.

"With sugar on it?"

Grinning from ear to ear, Angela spun around and raced back to Steve. Almost breathless, she told him the news. "Pam said you could help if you've a mind to."

"If I've a mind to? Are you kidding? Of course I've a mind to. How in the world did you ever pull that off?"

84

Afraid that Steve might hug her, Angela backed away. At one time, she would have welcomed his embrace. Now, things were different. Aside from feeling awkward, it might cause problems with Monica.

"Ahh shucks," she drawled, "it tweren't nuttin'."

"It certainly is," argued Steve. "In one afternoon you've accomplished what I couldn't in six months. You're marvelous. How can I ever thank you?"

"Share the harvest?" Her request was almost a whisper.

"What?" Steve looked puzzled.

Angela spread her arms. The area Steve had already tilled was almost an acre and the area he planned for potatoes would be at least that much. "This garden looks big enough to feed everyone in the hollow. And then some. When the crops start coming in, maybe you could give some to me and Gil."

Steve scratched his head and tried to look stern. "Okay, but you've got to help with the weeding." When he saw Angela's reaction, he laughed. "Just kidding," he roared. "There'll be more than enough for everyone. That was the whole idea of making it so large."

"Aha," snapped Angela. "The good preacher is trying to win souls with produce.

Pretty sneaky if you ask me."

Steve's expression turned serious. "Part of the reason for moving here was to help the disadvantaged. Prayers may fill the soul but it takes food to fill the belly. Did you know that most of the people in this hollow don't even have indoor plumbing?"

"No, I didn't. How do they manage without it?"

"They've got outhouses and they bathe in the river when the weather is warm enough."

The thought of jumping into a cold river sent chills down Angela's spine. "What do they do in the winter?"

"They use washtubs or take sponge baths. Sometimes they just do without."

"Wow. I never realized life was so tough out here."

Steve nodded and smiled. "Except for a few men like J.B. who take care of the oil rigs, most of the others work in the coal mines or live off the land. There's a family out on the backside of the ridge . . . a mom and five little kids. The dad died last month in a mining accident and the mom is expecting another baby. I thought we could help out until she gets back on her feet."

Angela regretted her thoughtless remark. Sometimes she let her mouth get ahead of her brain. That would have to stop. "Sorry

86

about what I said earlier. I should have known it was something like that. What else can I do besides weeding?"

"Oh, that'll be a big help," replied Steve. "With all the rain we get here, weeds grow faster than the bugs can eat them. That's why I want to plant hot peppers. I'm going to grow everything organically. You know — no artificial fertilizers, herbicides or pesticides. When Monica and I were in Nicaragua, we were mostly involved in helping people build homes and teaching their children how to read. Unfortunately, we never learned much about farming. So, when we moved here, I bought a couple of gardening books and from what I've read, pepper juice makes an excellent insect repellant."

"Great idea. And I think I know exactly where to find the seeds."

As soon as she got home, Angela called Gelah. "Do you have any seed catalogs I can borrow?"

"Gracious, yes," the woman replied. "I may not put in a garden anymore but I'm still partial to looking at all the new seeds they come up with. Always makes me wonder whatever happened to all those old-fashioned tomatoes and beans I used to plant."

"I think they call them heirlooms now," replied Angela. "The seeds are hard to find but a couple seed companies are trying to bring them back. If you're coming to church tomorrow, could you possibly bring the catalogs? Otherwise, I'll run by your place and pick them up when I go to town next week."

"My next door neighbor is carrying me to church. You met her . . . Belinda Williams? She's such a sweet lady, always doing nice things like that. I'll bring the catalogs but I'm afraid I won't be able to spend much time with you. Belinda's grans are coming for dinner and she'll need to get home right quick."

"Monica's planned a really nice lunch for after the service. If you can stay, Gil and I will drive you home."

Gelah's response was almost predictable. "Well, I'd hate to put you out."

"It would be our honor." Steve was right. She was starting to sound like a local.

At Sunday's service, Steve talked about families and gardens. "Raising a family is like planting a garden. You plant the seeds and hope for the best. As the tender seedlings grow, you nourish, cultivate and protect them from the outside world. You encourage them to reach for the sky and, once they can stand on their own, you support them when they need it. You watch them bloom and when they finally reach maturity, you take pleasure in what they offer."

Steve's words made Angela think about her daughter. Her birthday was a month away. How old would she be now? Forty-two? Forty-three? What did she look like? What was she doing? Was she married? Did she have children? All these years, Angela told herself she did the right thing by giving her child up. But she always wondered . . . Did she?

After the service, everyone headed for lunch at Steve and Monica's house. Since there were so few people, everyone fit comfortably around the dining room table. Monica and Steve sat at opposite ends, Gil and Angela on one side and Gelah and a woman from out on the hardtop on the other. Monica had prepared enough roast beef, brown gravy, mashed potatoes, and whole kernel corn for ten people. Whatever was left over would be sent home with Gelah and the other woman.

"I liked the way you compared seeds and children," commented Gelah. "I never thought of it that way but what you said made good sense. Especially the part about protecting the seedlings from the outside world. Nowadays there are so many dangers out there that young plants and children hardly stand a chance. Pollution and weak soil poison plants and television and computers destroy children's minds. I don't know how parents keep up anymore."

"That's why God created grandparents," joked Steve. "Whatever the parents can't handle, the grandparents take care of."

Directing his attention across the table, Gilberto asked, "My wife has told me you raised a large family. Is that correct, Mrs. Spears?"

"Oh, please, call me Gelah. And yes, I had four sons, Matthew, Mark, Luke and John and two daughters, Mary and Elizabeth."

"Do they live around here?" asked Gilberto.

"No. They all went to school and moved away. I guess there wasn't much to keep them in the hollows. Young people nowadays need more entertainment and excitement than they can find out here. And most of them don't seem all that interested in working the land. I'm afraid the days of living on the family farm are coming to an end. Matthew and Luke work with computers, Mark is a lawyer and John is an accountant." She seemed almost sad talking about her children.

"What about your daughters?" asked Monica.

"Elizabeth died in childbirth and Mary is somewhere in California. I haven't heard from her in years."

Sensing Gelah's sorrow, Angela asked about the foster children. "You took in twenty, didn't you?"

"Something like that," she replied. "They were the joy of my life. I never really kept count."

"Were they all local children?" asked Steve.

"No. Some were from West Virginia but others were from as far away as Kentucky, Tennessee and Ohio."

"What was it like raising someone else's children?" asked Monica.

"I never really thought about it," replied Gelah. "For whatever reason, God led those children to me and I treated them like my own. They were praised when they did good and punished when they did bad."

Angela remained silent as everyone continued asking Gelah about her foster children. Steve's sermon had started her thinking about her daughter. Now, she couldn't stop. From what she knew, the child had been adopted within days of her birth. But what if she had been placed in foster care? Would she have been fortunate enough to live with someone as warm and loving as Gelah?

As if reading her mind, Gilberto gently placed his arm around Angela's shoulder. It was a gesture she had grown accustomed to and it always made her feel protected and loved. With Gilberto by her side, she felt strong enough to ask, "Did you ever think about adopting any of them?"

Gilberto's hand tightened on Angela's shoulder but he didn't say a word.

"Yes, I thought about it," replied Gelah. "But I didn't want any of them to think I was trying to replace their real parents so I never did anything. Their young lives had been tough enough, I didn't need to cause them more pain. Besides, I couldn't have loved them any more if I'd adopted them."

All the talk of children and adoption made Angela uncomfortable. Just the thought of someone else raising the only child she ever had made her heart ache. She quickly changed the subject. "Did everyone see Steve's garden?"

"È meraviglioso," replied Gilberto. "I hope you will plant enough tomatoes for marinara."

"Don't worry, Gil. I ordered four dozen plants from the co-op."

"Four dozen?" It was the first time the woman from the hardtop had spoken during the entire meal. Her voice was shrill and school-marmish. "Why so many?"

"I wanted to have enough to share." Steve responded like a mischievous boy caught playing hooky.

"You'll do that alright. I get a bushel off-a each one-a my plants. Whaddaya gonna do with all the toe-maters you cain't give away?"

"Guess I hadn't really thought that far ahead. Any suggestions?"

For the next thirty minutes, everyone offered Steve advice as to what to do with the inevitable nightshade bumper crop. Gelah said she had canning jars he could use; Gilberto suggested making tomato paste; and Angela asked if there was a farmer's market anywhere in the area. There were also lots of tips about growing tomatoes. "Make sure you pinch off the bottom leaves." "Put brown paper bags or old toilet paper rolls around the stems to keep out the cutworms." "Plant carrots and garlic between the plants to keep pests down." "Don't forget to trim the suckers." When the dining room clock chimed two, everyone seemed surprised.

"Good grief, will you look at that?" gasped the hardtop lady. "I better get home 'fore someone comes lookin' fer me."

"Oh, my," stammered Gelah. "I've taken up so much of everyone's time already. I really feel terrible about having to ask for a ride home."

"Don't worry, Gelah," reassured Angela. "Gil and I will enjoy the ride."

Gilberto shook his head. "You look tired, amore mio. I will drive Miss Gelah to Pawpaw and you can get some rest. When I return, I will prepare dinner tonight so that you do not need to do anything."

For as much as Angela didn't want to admit it, Gilberto was right. She felt a little drained and didn't look forward to either a long ride or cooking dinner. Gil was a wonderful husband and she loved him for his considerate ways. And to think, she once thought of him as, how did her brother put it? *An aging lothario who came on to all the women?* She gave him a kiss and told him to hurry back.

"Si, mia bella moglie." he whispered.

Angela smiled as Gil and Gelah drove away. It felt good knowing she could finally trust a man.

7
Paintin' Day

Spring in West Virginia was beautiful but unpredictable. One day might be shirtsleeve weather, the next, three inches of snow could be on the ground. When Angela woke that Saturday morning, it was raining and the temperature was a full twenty degrees colder than the previous morning.

"Good grief, Gil, look at this." She was standing at the bedroom window trying to sop up raindrops that had worked their way through the weathered frame. Some of the drops trailed down the window, froze on their journey and created frosty dreamscapes.

"It is nothing but rain, *amore mio*. Do not soil your robe, I will get a towel."

Angela leaned her forehead against the cold, damp glass and sighed. "How are we going to paint the church if this rain keeps up?"

"Maybe we could paint the inside," suggested Gilberto.

Dressing quickly, Angela rushed downstairs while Gilberto cleaned up the window. Even though she thought her husband was the world's most talented cook, she enjoyed making his breakfast every morning. She'd even developed a rotating menu so she wouldn't serve him the same thing twice in one week. Her recipes weren't as unique as her husband's but they filled the void created after a long night's sleep. Saturday's special was egg-in-a-hole, a one-pan wonder she'd perfected while still living in Kokomo.

When they first moved into the house on the ridge, there was a wood burning stove in the kitchen. Even though Angela favored the idea of old-timey cooking, she quickly learned of its difficulties, especially the part about adding too much wood and burning whatever she was trying to cook. Gil and Steve made an emergency trip to the trading post, found a battered stove, without all the bells and whistles as Monica's but serviceable nonetheless, fixed it up and installed it in the kitchen. It had four burners and ran on natural gas that was free because the farm's original owners had sold the land's mineral rights to the oil company and were given full use of as much gas as they, or any subsequent owners, could ever use. The only problem was the burners were old and had to be lit whenever someone wanted to use them.

Angela reached for the safety matches, took one out of the box, flicked it with a fingernail and lit the burner. The stove immediately came to life. She positioned a black iron frying pan on one of the front burners, added canola oil and placed three slices of homemade potato bread in the sizzling pan. She knew butter would have been tastier but she was trying to reduce Gilberto's fat intake. Men like him were hard to find and she was determined to do everything in her power to keep him around for a long time to come.

When one side of the bread was nicely toasted, she flipped it over, carved a hole in the center and cracked an egg over the hole. Unlike store-bought eggs, the bright yellow yolks stood tall in the pan instead of spreading against the bottom. She smiled at the sight — just another advantage to living in the country.

Gilberto walked into the room and wrapped his arm around Angela's waist. "Hmm, *delizioso*. Shall I pour the juice?"

"Yes, please." Angela placed two egg-in-a-holes on Gilberto's plate and one on her own. After adding fresh berries she'd found growing in the garden, she moved the plates to the table and invited Gilberto to eat. *"Mangia, mangia,"* she ordered.

"Oh, my darling wife," scolded Gilberto, "after six months of marriage, you still do not speak Italian? It is *mangiare* not *mangia.*"

Knowing she would get a sympathetic response, Angela covered her eyes and pretended to cry.

"Sono spiacente," begged Gilberto. "Please, *non piangere.*"

Revealing her eyes and a toothy grin, Angela begged her husband to translate.

"I just said that I am sorry," he replied. "I did not mean to make you cry. But of course, now that I see you are not crying, maybe it is you who should be apologizing."

Angela gave Gilberto a quick peck on the cheek and signaled for him to sit down. A frown spread across her face as she picked at her egg. "I'm worried that if the rain doesn't stop no one will show up and we'll never be able to get them back in the church."

Gilberto reached across the table and gently patted his wife's hand. "While I was drying off the window I noticed the sun breaking through the clouds. It is only eight o'clock but I am sure that by ten, the rain will have stopped and the sun will be shining. You will see . . . everything will be fine."

By the time Gilberto and Angela arrived at the church, Pam and her two sons were already setting up their ladders. As predicted, the sun was out, the outside walls of the church were dry and, except for a little mud, it looked like the weather was going to be perfect for painting.

Turning from her sons, Pam announced that she had invited several other neighbors. "Not sure how many will show," she shouted, "but I figured the more hands the better."

"Good thinking." Jumping from his truck, Steve quickly ran around to the back, lowered the tailgate and started dragging paint cans across the truck bed floor. He was wearing an old *Gators* sweatshirt and paint-splattered jeans. Angela wondered if those were the same jeans he'd worn while painting her house.

Steve shouted to Gilberto. "Hey Gil, wanna help with these?"

While Steve and Gilberto were unloading the supplies, two more pickups pulled into the yard. One carried Sharon and Randy Schuster and their two girls, the other Gelah and a young man Angela had never seen before. Strapped to the cab of the young man's truck were two more ladders. That made twelve workers and four ladders. More than enough to get the job done. The two people conspicuously absent were J.B. and Monica.

"Where's Monica?" asked Angela.

"Home with a headache," replied Steve. "She gets them a lot whenever the barometer drops."

Angela wondered if the headache had anything to do with Monica's recent mood change. But, deciding it was better not to discuss it right there and then, she simply asked, "Will she be all right?"

"Sure," replied Steve. "You know her . . . she's tough." Cutting off further conversation, Steve grabbed two paint cans and walked away from his truck. His abrupt departure made Angela wonder if there was more to Monica's absence than a mere headache.

Pam's oldest son grabbed the paint cans from Steve's hands and tossed one to his brother. "We don't gotta pray or nuttin' 'fore we begin, do we?" asked the younger boy.

"Only if you want to." Steve laughed and walked away.

The Walton boys climbed to the top of their ladders and started painting the underside of the eaves while Sharon's girls stood below and giggled. The as-yet-unidentified young man stationed his ladders one at the front and one at the rear of the church. Angela walked up to Gelah and asked who the stranger was.

"One of my fosters," replied the woman. "His name is Peter. When I told him we were going to paint the church, he called a couple of my other foster kids and tried to talk them into coming as well. Problem was they already had plans. Said they would run by next week if we don't finish today."

"They keep in touch with one another?"

"Oh, yes. Most foster children do."

Gilberto tapped Angela on the shoulder. "I am sorry to interrupt," he said, "but Miss Pamela says she needs your advice."

"Pam needs advice from me?" Angela excused herself and hurried toward the rear of the church where Pam stood looking toward the woods. She was holding something in her hands.

"What's that?" asked Angela.

"A piece of copper tubing," mumbled Pam.

Sounding like a conspirator caught in a cloak-and-dagger scheme, Angela whispered, "Is that so unusual?"

"Only if it belongs to a still."

"A still? Like in moonshine?" Angela found it hard not to laugh. Stills and moonshiners had gone the way of the Hatfields and McCoys — hadn't they?

"Yes," replied Pam. "Moonshine. Think we should tell the preacher?"

"One piece of pipe doesn't mean much. Maybe we should look around and see if we find anything else."

Without warning, J.B. slithered from behind a tree and approached his wife. "No need lookin' fer nuttin' else," he hissed. "That there pipe must'a fell off'a my truck when I was out back checking wells."

"What are you doing out here, J.B. Walton?" Pam looked and sounded angry. "I thought you went to town for tractor parts."

"Been there and back," he replied sullenly. "Didn' have nuttin' I wanted."

"Well, all right then. Grab a paintbrush and get to work."

"Ain't never gonna happen, woman," growled J.B. "I tol you afore. I don't want no part'a this place. An you shouldn' neither. I've haffa mind to drag ya' back to the house right this minute."

Pam stood her ground and shouted into J.B.'s face. Tiny shards of spittle accompanied her words. "What's stopping you?"

"Got somewhere else ta be." J.B. vanished

into the trees before Pam could stop him.

"Wow," exclaimed Angela. "What was that all about?"

"Don't pay any attention to him," replied Pam. "He gets kind of cranky when things don't go his way."

"Is he mad because you're here?"

"Yes, but I don't care." Pam shrugged her shoulders and returned to painting.

Realizing their conversation was over, Angela started walking back to the front of the church but stopped, turned and asked Pam, "So, why *did* you come?"

Without stopping work, Pam replied. "I used to come to this old church when I was a little girl. In fact, this is where my parents were married and where I was saved." Her words were soft and almost wistful. "It was a nice place back then and I always felt comfortable here. If it was fixed up all proper like, I'd probably start coming again."

"Really? Does Steve know?" Angela was so excited she practically shrieked.

"Preacher Steve? No, I haven't told him. Thought I'd wait and see if he's really as nice as people says he is."

"People are saying he's nice? I thought no one liked him."

Pam put her paintbrush down. "Oh, that's

just our way. We measure a person up before we decide if we like them or not. So far, the preacher's been pretty straight with everyone. I hear he's even helping that Widow Putnam over in Looneyville. Seems the only one that doesn't like him is J.B."

"Why is that?" asked Angela.

"I'm not sure," replied Pam. "He just keeps telling me and the boys to keep away from this church. Something about it not being a safe place to be."

Angela couldn't believe her ears. "That's the whole reason for fixing it up. We want it to be safe and comfortable so that people will enjoy coming here, just like you did when you were a child."

Instead of returning to the front of the church, Angela hung back with Pam and helped her paint the wall nearest the woods. She probably didn't have anything to worry about but it just seemed smarter to stay with Pam in case J.B. came back. He hadn't looked too happy. There was no telling what he might do. Besides, Gilberto and Gelah were working on the double front doors, Gelah's foster son and Steve were on ladders painting the windows, Sharon and Randy were halfway through the west wall and Pam's boys and Sharon's girls seemed to have the east wall under control. If the weather held and the pace kept up, the work would be done before midday.

Monica arrived shortly before noon with a five-gallon jug of lemonade and a basket filled with sandwiches and fresh fruit. "Is anyone hungry?" she yelled.

Steve jumped from his ladder and ran to help her. "How's your headache?" His question seemed sincere and Monica seemed to soften beneath his gentle concern.

"I'm fine," she replied. "All I needed was a little rest." She started pouring lemonade while Steve handed out the sandwiches.

"Can I help?" asked Angela.

"Sure, take a couple of these over to Gil and Gelah."

Angela picked up two paper cups and walked toward Gilberto and Gelah who appeared to be having a serious conversation. As she got closer, the conversation stopped. Angela wondered if they were talking about her. Ever since Easter dinner, Gilberto had been spending a lot of time with Gelah. He volunteered to drive her home whenever she needed a lift after church and he was always running errands for her. Angela knew she was probably being paranoid but what if Gil was attracted to Gelah? After all, Gelah was closer to his age than she was. She took a deep breath and tried to hide her suspicions as she handed Gilberto his drink.

"Is everything all right?" he asked. "You look concerned."

"I'm fine," she lied. "It's just that Pam and J.B. had a little disagreement and I'm worried it isn't over yet."

Gilberto swallowed his lemonade in one gulp. "Where is she? I will go and make sure no harm comes to her."

Angela watched as Gilberto hurried away. She wanted to believe she didn't have any reason to worry about him but she'd once trusted Carl and look how that turned out. *No,* she screamed to herself, *this can't be happening again.*

"Maybe you should sit down," suggested Gelah.

The touch of the older woman's hand on her shoulder shocked Angela back to reality. "What were you two talking about?" She wasn't sure where she'd found the courage to ask the question, all she knew was the words were out of her mouth before she could think about what she was saying or how she was saying it.

Showing no sign of being offended by the rude outburst, Gelah picked up her paintbrush and went back to work. "Your husband asked if I knew where he could buy goats. He said you'd had them when you were growing up and that you might like to have some again."

Gelah's answer sounded believable and Angela regretted thinking anything bad about Gilberto. He was a good and decent man and would never cheat on her. His main concern had always been her and now he was even thinking about buying goats just to make her happy. Feeling like a heavy burden had been lifted from her shoulders, Angela clamped her hands over her mouth and giggled. "Goats? Really?"

"That's what he said," replied Gelah.

Even though she felt like running after and hugging her husband, Angela decided to stay where she was and finish painting where he'd left off. There would be time enough to thank him for his thoughtfulness later in the evening. Right now, there was work to do.

With so many hands to share the job, the painting was finished before three. Steve and Monica thanked everyone for their hard work and invited them to the Sunday service. "I won't preach if you don't want me to. Maybe we'll just have coffee and donuts."

Some of the adults nodded while the teenagers examined their shoes. Angela wondered if anyone other than Gelah would show up. Maybe it was too soon. Maybe they needed more time to get used to the new church. And the preacher.

As they were walking back to their truck, Angela grabbed Gilberto's hand. "Gelah told me what you two were talking about."

"She did?" Gilberto looked shocked.

"Yes. The goats."

"Oh. *Sì, sì.* The goats."

"Can we really get some? If we had a couple females we could milk them and if we got at least one male we could start a whole herd." Angela didn't try to hide her excitement.

"A herd?" asked Gilberto. "I thought we might start with one or two and see what happens."

"Oh, we'll need more than just one or two," argued Angela. "A lactating female will produce about five pounds of milk a day. That's a little more than half-a-gallon, a lot less if she's nursing. Considering how much we'll have to pay for dairy feed, hay and medical supplies, we should get enough females so we can sell the milk."

"Really?" Gilberto grinned and leaned against the truck. "And who is going to do all this milking?"

"We could take turns. I could do the morning milking and you could do the evening. Or the other way around." Angela climbed into the truck, leaned across the seat and opened the driver's side door for Gilberto.

"They must be milked twice each day?" Gilberto got in the truck but didn't start the engine.

"Every twelve hours. If you don't they could get sick."

"It sounds like a lot of work."

Angela punched Gilberto's shoulder. "I thought Gelah told you all about goats."

"Just where to buy them, not how to milk them." Starting the engine, he slowly pulled away from the church.

"Well, never mind," replied Angela. "I'll teach you everything you need to know."

Gilberto laughed. "Hmm, that sounds interesting."

"It will be," promised Angela. "It will be."

8
GIRL TALK

Aside from Gelah, five people showed up for the Sunday service. It wasn't a crowd but at least it was progress in the right direction. Although Steve looked pleased with the turnout, Monica hardly acknowledged anyone's presence. She didn't take part in the service, she didn't join in the songs, in fact, all she did was keep her eyes lowered and shoulders slumped.

While everyone else bustled around vying for Steve's attention, Angela took hold of Monica's arm and walked her outside.

"Where are you taking me?" demanded Monica.

Angela squeezed Monica's arm tighter. "It's such a beautiful day. I thought a walk along the river might be nice."

After Saturday's rain, the surrounding forest was alive in delicate shades of green, purple, yellow and pink. The serviceberry, or *sarvis* as all the locals called it, had lost

110

its droopy white flowers but was showing signs of developing the juicy dark fruit Gelah said made such excellent wine. High on the slopes, black walnut trees hid their globular fruit for now but would eagerly drop them when the weather cooled in the fall. Tender shoots of poke sallet reached for the sun. Their leaves might be good fried or parboiled but once the berries appeared, the plant would be toxic.

A red-breasted robin pecked for worms and, although she didn't see it, Angela identified the raucous call of a blackbird as it attended its nest in the rushes. "It's beautiful here, isn't it?" she asked.

Monica sighed and stared vacantly into space.

For a while, the two women walked along the river in silence. Water striders were already skating across the surface; it wouldn't be long before dragonflies joined them.

Spotting a fallen tree, Angela motioned for Monica to sit. "We need to talk."

"About what?" snapped Monica.

"You." Worried her questions might anger Monica, Angela spoke softly as she sat on the log. "Is everything all right?"

"If you don't mind, I'd rather not talk about it."

Monica's answer was like a dagger in Angela's chest but she bit her lower lip and continued. "It might make you feel better."

"What do you care how I feel?" Monica hung her head and began to sob.

Angela wrapped her arms around the weeping woman and tried to console her. "Of course I care. Without you I'd probably still be killing bugs and dodging hurricanes back in Florida."

"Maybe we'd all be better off there." Monica pulled away from Angela and wiped her tears with her shirtsleeve.

"What do you mean," asked Angela. "Don't you like it here?"

"I hate it," bellowed Monica. "It's always raining, the people are deceitful and belligerent, and if there was an emergency no one would ever make it down that poor excuse of a road. I feel like I'm living on a foreign planet or something."

"Come on, Monica, it's not that bad."

"No? Did Steve ever tell you about the time he had to drive one of the neighbors to the hospital?"

"No, he didn't. When was that?"

"Shortly after we moved here." Monica stood up and started walking back and forth in front of the downed tree. "It seems old man Boggs lived in this hollow his entire life. Literally. He never went away to school, held a job or went into town for supplies. Said everything he needed was right here. Whatever he couldn't kill, grow or trade for, he didn't need. He lived back off the road on his family's run-down farm, had no electric or indoor plumbing and never owned a truck or car. Somewhere along the way, he married one of his not-too-distant cousins and raised a couple of kids. Everyone thought he was a little crazy, including his kids. When they grew up they moved away and left him high and dry." Monica took a deep breath before continuing her tirade. "Well, lo and behold, one day the old man has a heart attack and no one is willing to go in after him except my big-hearted husband who jumps in his truck, rescues the guy from his ramshackle house and drives him to the hospital."

"That's wonderful," exclaimed Angela.

"That's what most people would say," replied Monica, "but old man Boggs didn't see it that way. No sirree. On the drive into town, he was in so much pain all he could do was groan. But once he felt better, he started swearing at Steve saying that he had no right to drag him from his home and, as he put it, 'subject him to the inhumane brutalities of modern medicine.' "

"He said that?"

"Those were his exact words."

"How'd he get so educated?"

"Who cares?" Monica stopped pacing, placed both hands on her hips and glared at Angela. "The point is, the people out here don't want our help and they most certainly don't want us here."

"That's not true," argued Angela. "Look at how everyone helped out yesterday. They'd do anything for you and Steve."

"No, Angela, they did it for you, not me and Steve."

"Oh, Monica, how can you say that?"

"Because it's true." Monica started crying again. "You're like a Midas or something. Everything you touch turns to gold. You moved to Florida, turned your life around and ended up marrying the best catch in the park. Then you moved here and talked all the women into making curtains."

"It was only two." Angela tried to make light of her efforts.

"What difference does that make? Bottom line is you brought more people to the church than I ever could. I tried talking to people and they turned away. I tried to start a Sunday school and no one came. I even invited people to dinner and all they did was eat my food and run. I'm such a loser. I

114

should never have come here."

Monica tried to walk away but Angela grabbed her wrist. "Wait a minute," she begged. "You're not a loser."

"Yes I am." Monica moaned and struggled to free her hand. "I've never been able to help anyone."

"What about all those people in Nicaragua? What about Florida? You helped a lot of people there, didn't you?"

Monica tuned and faced Angela. "Steve helped them. Not me. I just rode on his shirttails."

Over the years, Angela had read enough women's magazines to guess what was really wrong with Monica. "How old are you, Monica?" she asked.

"Fifty-nine. But what does that have to do with anything?" Monica frowned. Because she wasn't wearing makeup, her crow's-feet and age spots stood out like red flags. Coarse dark hairs sprouted from her chin.

Knowing it was better to tread lightly, Angela cautiously replied. "Well, when women get to a certain age, strange things start to happen."

Monica laughed. "You mean menopause? I went through that years ago."

"Well, maybe you're experiencing post-menopausal problems," replied Angela.

"Like what?" Monica practically shouted.

"Headaches, lack of energy, difficulty sleeping, depression, and high blood pressure to name a few."

Monica walked back to the log and sat down. "Has Steve been complaining about me?" She whimpered and hung her head again.

"Of course not," replied Angela. "It's just that I went through a lot of those things myself. In fact, there were times I felt like I was coming apart at the seams."

"So what'd you do?"

"I went to a doctor."

"And what did he do? Put you on hormones or something?"

"We talked about it," replied Angela. "But when I told him I didn't want to take drugs, he told me to get more exercise and change my diet. He even convinced me to give up smoking."

"That's it?"

"Well, no. He also suggested I get a hobby. Said I needed to have a focus other than myself."

"A hobby? You think I need a hobby?" Monica's tolerance was wearing thin.

"Sure. Why not? Gil and I are going to look at some goats this afternoon. Why don't you come along? It might take your mind off whatever's bothering you."

Later that afternoon, Gilberto pulled his truck into a farm fifteen miles outside the hollow. The house was in worse condition than Steve and Monica's, but the satellite dish and showroom-new truck out back were sure signs the people living inside weren't poor.

As Gilberto parked the truck, Angela noticed an old barn with a large corral enclosed by three rows of thin wires. While everyone got out of the truck and started walking toward the house, a herd of Toggenburg goats burst from the barn and ran toward the edge of the corral. Staying a safe distance from the wires, they bayed and bleated for attention.

"Will you look at that?" squealed Monica. "Goats."

As everyone hurried toward the goats, a raspy voice cautioned them, "Watch out fer them wyrs. They be lec-tree-fried."

Steve spread his arms to stop the others from going any further. "Be careful," he warned. "I saw a dog jump one of those fences once and I'm sure it was an experience he never repeated."

"You the folks what wanted ta buy some goats?" The voice belonged to a tall, skinny man with graying hair. His threadbare clothes hung loosely on his scarecrow frame. "Wondered if you'd show." Scratching his underarm, he spit brown liquid on the ground.

Stepping around the fluid mess, Gilberto approached the man. "Our friend, Gelah Spears, told us you might have goats for sale."

"Yup," The man rubbed his hands together. "How many ya want?"

"I don't know," mused Angela. "How many do you want, Monica?"

"Me? I thought we came here to buy *you* some goats. I never said anything about wanting one." Monica's startled expression made everyone laugh.

"True," agreed Angela. "But since Gil and I are going to get a couple, I thought you might like to get some as well. You know . . . for a hobby?"

"Whaddaya plan to do wit' 'em," asked the farmer. "Milk 'em or eat 'em?"

"Milk them," exclaimed Angela. "I could never bring myself to eating an animal I raised."

"What are ya? One-a-dem veg-er-tear-e-ans?" The man scratched himself again.

"Not exactly." Angela took two steps back. If the man had fleas, she didn't want to take any home to Gizmo. "It's just that most of the animals I've owned have been like pets."

"Don't know much 'bout the country, do ya?" The man snickered.

Straightening his shoulders, Gilberto came to Angela's defense. "My wife grew up on a farm in Indiana. I can assure you, sir, she knows as much about the country as you do. She was in 4-H."

Steve pushed his way between Gilberto and the farmer. "How 'bout we get two males and two females? That way, each of the girls can have a breeding pair."

"Better off with one male and three females," argued the man. "That way, you'll get more milk. Sides, if a buck be worth his feed, he'll get all the females good and proper, if ya know what I mean."

Monica blushed but didn't say a word.

"He's right," agreed Angela. "And if we have one herd instead of two, we can keep them in one place and share the responsibility of caring for them."

"Makes sense to me," added Steve. "So how do we do this? Do we just pick out the ones we want, or what?"

The man's demeanor changed, probably because he knew he was making a sale. "The ones with collars be mine," he said. "Other than that, take whichever ones ya want. Onct ya make yur choice, I'll load 'em on'ta yur truck."

"Okay, ladies," chuckled Steve. "Go to it."

After the farmer showed them a safe way into the corral, Angela and Monica ran from goat to goat, checking them out, trying to determine which were the cutest and friendliest, and seemingly having the time of their lives. One of the goats with horn buds developing on his head butted Monica. "Whoa," she yelled, "quit picking on me, buster."

Angela was on the other side of the corral but ran toward Monica when she heard the ruckus. "That's a male." She spoke with an air of confidence. "And it looks like he likes you."

"Gee," Monica rubbed her rear. "How could you tell?"

"You know, as aggressive as he seems, he'll probably make a good stud."

"Good grief, Angela. Must you be so crude?"

"I'm just telling it like it is," Angela chuckled, then skipping backwards, hurried back to the other side of the pen.

An hour later four chocolate-brown goats were loaded into the back of Gilberto's truck. Not wanting to take the chance of any of them jumping out, Angela and Monica climbed in with the animals. Then, each hanging onto the necks of two goats, they discussed what was going to happen next.

Angela was full of ideas. "For the time being, we can put them in your old tractor shed but the boys are going to have to build a secure fence and probably some sort of milking barn pretty quick."

Monica jumped right in. "Maybe we could get some of the neighbors to help in exchange for milk."

"Good idea. And maybe they could show us what to do with the milk."

"You don't know?" Monica looked surprised.

"No," replied Angela. "I only raised males. We used them instead of lawn mowers."

"Males?" Monica screeched loud enough to startle the goats.

"Hush up," whispered Angela. "I don't want Gilberto to know. He thinks I know everything there is to know about farming."

"Aha," teased Monica. "I'm gonna tell."

"Don't you dare," pleaded Angela. One of the goats started chewing on her shirt collar. "Cut that out," she squealed.

Monica grinned. "What'sa matter, farmer lady? Is that little ol' goat pickin' on ya?"

"You're enjoying this, aren't you?" hissed Angela.

"As a matter of fact I am," replied Monica. "It's the most fun I've had in a long time. Thanks so much for kicking me in the rear."

"I think the goat did that . . . not me." Angela laughed and tried to tuck the damp collar inside her shirt. The goat pulled it back out and went back to chewing. Realizing it was a lost cause, she let the animal have its way. "By the way, have you thought about what you're going to name your goats?"

"They have to have names?"

"Of course," replied Angela. "How else are they going to know which one we're talking to?"

"We're going to talk to them?" Monica's smile spread from ear to ear. "How will we know if they understand us?"

"Easy," replied Angela. "They'll answer us. One *baaaa* is for yes, two is for no."

Steve turned around and stuck his head out the back cab window. "Hey, you two. What's going on back there?"

"Nothing much," answered Monica. "We're just talkin'." She winked at Angela as the truck bounced down the washboard road.

9
THE GREAT ESCAPE

Because of rain-forest-like humidity, the early-June garden was yielding enough crops to feed all the raccoons, rabbits, box turtles and groundhogs that followed their noses or snouts to it. Luckily, there were always vegetables enough left over for the humans.

After bringing the goats home, Steve and Gilberto fenced in a two-acre plot downwind from the house and built an open-sided pole barn that kept the hay and dairy feed dry and provided a secure place for the goats to sleep. Off to one side, an oversized aluminum shed purchased from the farm co-op acted as a temporary milking barn. Inside, a warped wooden door set on recycled cinder blocks functioned as a milking stanchion. If the goats produced surplus milk and there was a market for it, a large health-inspector-approved barn and a more substantial stanchion would have to be built. Until then, the makeshift structures served their purpose.

Having settled in to their new surroundings, the three does, Sophia, Dolly, and Marilyn, were producing a minimum of three gallons a day. Once collected, the milk was strained through cheesecloth, pasteurized to kill any bacteria and quickly refrigerated until someone, usually Gilberto, found time to whip up a batch of cheese. His favorite was a velvety blend of fresh herbs, olive oil and wine — perfect for smearing on homemade Italian bread.

Since the men shied away from the task, Angela and Monica took turns milking the goats. One week Angela took the morning shift and Monica the evening; the next week they switched. That way, each woman got an opportunity to sleep in, if only every other week.

Monica seemed to love her new role as goat farmer. Even when it wasn't her turn, she spent time with the animals, brushed them, trimming their hooves and yanking out any harmful weeds growing in their fenced-off area. She often bragged that the *girls* gave more milk when she did the milking. Even though Angela didn't believe a word of it, she never argued the point. Nor did she ask Monica whether she had seen a doctor. Somehow, it didn't matter if her friend was taking drugs or not. All she needed to know was that her outlook on life had improved and she was smiling a lot more lately.

One morning, while working in the vegetable garden, Monica and Angela were startled by a deafening explosion coming from the hill behind the house. Shaking the earth and echoing through the hollow, it was followed by a second blast. And then a third.

"Good grief," shouted Monica. "They fired up Big Jake again."

Angela cupped her hands and shouted back. "Who's that?"

The noise stopped suddenly. "It's not a who, it's a what." Monica rubbed her ears and lowered her voice. "Remember the night you met Pam and J.B. and they told that crazy story about Jake and Bertha Withers?"

"You mean the people who used to own this farm?"

"Yeah. Them. Well, folks around here believe that if the oil company hadn't put in any wells, Jake Withers might still be alive. They say he was so obsessed with money that he spent all his time at his wells, especially the one on the hill where they found his body. In fact, they even say his wife died because he never had time for her."

"Poor thing." Angela shook her head. After being neglected by her first husband, she knew how that could feel.

"It all started when Withers found out some of his wells had to be closed down because they weren't producing enough crude. I guess he thought if he worked harder on the remaining wells, they'd make up for the ones that were closed, he'd make more money and his wife would be happy. But, of course, that never happened. Anyway, one by one, the oil company continued to close down his wells and, by the time Bertha was gone, all he had left was one. Then the oil company decided to close that one down too, so he pumped it, oiled it and replaced all the old parts himself. When Jake's body was found wrapped around that well, people started calling it Big Jake's Well or just Big Jake. They say that, to this day, the old man walks the woods looking for someone to start that well up again. And, at least once a year, someone does."

"That's ridiculous."

There was another explosion. Monica frowned and pulled the bandana she was wearing over her ears to block the noise. "Tell them that."

As usual, Gizmo had spent most of the morning napping in the sun. The first blast didn't faze him but when it kept happening, he woke up. Rising from his comfortable spot on the freshly turned soil, he stretched, yawned and turned his head just in time to see the goats break loose from their pen. Angela and Monica spotted them, too, but it was Gizmo who reacted quickly and tore off after the runaways.

The goats sprinted across the fields and raced down the slope toward the river. Hesitating for a split second when he neared the water, Bucky, the male, took the lead and thundered across the bridge. Dolly, Sophia, Marilyn and Gizmo were in close pursuit. Once across the bridge, the animals disappeared into the woods.

Angela panicked. "What do we do now?"

"How should I know," blared Monica. "You're the one that's supposed to know all about goats."

Gathering her wits, Angela snapped into action. "Take the Jeep and head up to the ridge. I'll go through the woods and try to steer them towards you."

"What do I do once they get there?" asked Monica.

"I haven't figured that out yet," confessed Angela.

As Monica sped off in the topless Jeep, Angela tromped across the bridge. Because she'd been gardening, she was wearing cutoffs and garden clogs . . . not the best attire for traipsing through the woods, but what choice did she have?

The morning sun hadn't penetrated the woods and the ground beneath the trees was covered with damp leaves. Angela tried to maintain her footing, but every time she picked up any speed, her feet slipped and she fell face first into the slime. She tried to break off a tree branch to use as a walking stick but ended up scraping the palms of her hands instead. Hearing Gizmo's barks and the goats bawling like frightened school-children, she ignored her bruises. She was afraid of the harm that might come to the animals, especially Gizmo. Having almost lost him to a hurricane, she took every precaution to protect her loyal friend.

At one point, Angela thought she saw one of the animals moving through the trees. But what if it was something else? What if it was a mountain lion? Or worse — a bear? Did the books say to stand still or run when you encountered a bear? She couldn't re-member.

Disregarding her own safety, she forged ahead. When she finally reached the top of the ridge, Monica was standing next to the Jeep waiting for her but neither Gizmo nor the goats were anywhere in sight.

"What happened to you?" howled Monica.

Looking down, Angela noticed she was wearing only one shoe and that both of her knees were covered in mud and bleeding. "I must have fallen." She spit on her hand and tried to rub some of the mud off her knees. In the process, she ground dirt into her wounds. "Ouch."

"Let's find you some shoes and get those knees taken care of," ordered Monica.

"What about Gizmo? And the goats?" Angela wiped a dirt-encrusted hand across her cheek. She was tired and wanted to sit down but knew she couldn't until all the animals were caught and returned home safely.

"I sent Gil to get Steve," said Monica. "They'll find them."

Monica's voice was soft and reassuring. It calmed Angela's nerves and gave her confidence that everything would turn out well. Had she learned that in the convent or did it come naturally? Could something like that come naturally? Angela wondered why she couldn't be like Monica. Not a nun necessarily, but someone who made other people feel better. Gave them something to hold on to. Eased their pain. Gave them hope.

After her divorce, Angela considered joining Vista but never did anything about it because she was afraid she wouldn't succeed. Everything she ever tried, including marriage, had been a failure. Why should volunteering to fight poverty be any different? Now, even though she was living the life she'd always dreamed about, she still didn't feel like she had accomplished anything. Raising goats was fun but there was something more that she could do. Something more she had to do. But what? She couldn't imagine how anything she might do would make a difference. But then, neither had she imagined she would be living in a renovated century-old house, living off the land, and listening to someone tell her that, even though the sky was falling, everything was going to be all right. She leaned against the Jeep and sighed. "Do you really think so?"

"Oh course," replied Monica.

From out of nowhere, the goats appeared, rushed past the Jeep, across the ridge and back into the woods. Gizmo was right behind them. Nipping at the runaways' heels and jogging from side to side, his head was hung low. He seemed to be herding the fugitive animals.

"Look at that," laughed Monica. "Where'd he learn that?"

Angela grinned. "I don't know. Maybe one of the neighbor dogs taught him."

By the time Angela and Monica returned to the farm, the men had everything under control. Steve was working on the fence, Gilberto was testing the battery and Gizmo was holding the goats at bay in the desecrated pen. Once Steve gave the signal that the fence was repaired, Gilberto turned the charger on. There were a few sparks and sizzles but everything seemed to be working properly. Knowing his work was done, Gizmo relaxed but never took his eyes off the goats.

As if sizing up his opponent, Bucky looked around before approaching the dog. His steps were slow and measured. The two males locked eyes. Bucky stomped the ground. Gizmo lowered his head. The battle began.

Although only a couple inches in length, Bucky's prepubescent horns made contact with Gizmo's skull. A dull, watermelon-thumping thud reverberated through the hills. Looking slightly dazed but unharmed,

Gizmo rammed his head full force into the goat's front legs. Bucky's knees buckled but he didn't fall. Rearing up on his hind legs, he curled his lip and took a running leap for Gizmo. Seeing it coming, Gizmo mimicked the move. Time and time again, they repeated the attack but, missing each other by a country mile, neither male ever made contact.

All of a sudden, Bucky lifted his tail, changed course and sprinted toward the log and plank teeter-totter set up at the far end of the pen. Flanked by the female goats, Gizmo followed.

With his head held high, Bucky took his position on one end of the plank while Sophia jumped on the board and walked toward the opposite end. As if knowing how to play the game, Gizmo jumped on the lowered plank. The board bounced up and down as the female walked back and forth between the two males. Gizmo shifted his weight from front to rear while Bucky seemed glued in place. All the while, the humans were watching.

"Who do you think's gonna win?" asked Steve.

Gilberto chuckled and slapped Steve's back. "The one with the biggest feet, of course."

Later that evening, Angela called Katherine to tell her about the day. "You should have seen Gizmo." She didn't try to hide the excitement and pride that filled her heart. "He chased those goats down and played with them like it was something he'd been doing his entire life."

"I wish I could have been there," replied Katherine.

Angela sighed and took a big breath. "You know, I really love it here but I miss you, too. I wish you could be here to share all of this with me."

"You know the way Mongo is. He loves the ocean. He'd be like a fish out of water up there."

Angela laughed. "Well, we've got a river. It isn't very deep but it's still water."

"Mongo's been talking a lot about Cuba lately." Katherine's tone turned serious. "Says he misses home and now that Steve and Gil are gone, he's got no one to hang out with."

"Why don't you come up for a visit? You never know, he might enjoy himself. I'm sure Gil and Steve would be happy to see him."

"Oh, I don't know. Things have been so expensive lately. We're trying to save our pennies."

Sensing that Katherine was looking for excuses, Angela refused to give in. "It wouldn't cost anything but gas. You could stay in the little trailer by the river and eat veggies fresh from the garden."

"What? No meat?"

"Well, maybe we could get the guys to go hunting."

"Gil hunts?"

"Not so much hunting as sightseeing. Last time he and Steve went out for quail, every time they flushed a flock, Gil just stood and watched the birds fly away. He said they were so beautiful he didn't have the heart to shoot them."

"Good thing you've got that garden. Otherwise, you'd starve."

Katherine asked how the goats were doing, Angela talked about how things were going at the church and then a strange voice broke into the conversation. "Why don' you tell her 'bout the Harvest Festival coming up?"

"Who's that?" demanded Katherine.

"Jist me," the voice replied. "Sharon Schuster. I'm one'a Angela's neighbors."

Angela wasn't surprised by the intrusion. "Hey, Sharon, how's it going? Thanks for reminding me about the festival. When is it again?"

"First part'a September — around Labor Day, I think. It's alotta fun . . . everyone goes."

Angela picked up Sharon's enthusiasm. "Yeah and from what I hear, there's arts and crafts, entertainment, fireworks, carnival rides and enough food to feed a small country. I think they even have an old-fashioned barbecue complete with roasted whole hogs."

"Charming." Katherine didn't sound impressed.

"Seriously. Think about it. We'd have so much fun . . . just like old times."

"I'd have to talk to Mongo."

"Please do. I want to show you and your wild hair off to all my neighbors."

Sharon broke in again. "Sumpin' wrong with her hair?"

"No," hissed Katherine. "It's red. Just like everyone else's."

"Mine ain't red. It be blonde."

"Whatever."

Aware that Katherine was annoyed with the rude interruptions, Angela asked Sharon if she needed to use the phone or was just being sociable.

"The TV quit workin' so I thought I'd call Ms. Hutchins up ta Ripley. Then I heard you two a-talkin' and decided ta listen in.

Ya don't mind, do ya?"

Katherine took a deep breath as if she was about to speak her mind but Angela cut her off. "No, we don't mind, Sharon. But next time you pick up, just let me know you're on the line. Okay?"

"I kin do that."

"Thanks, Sharon. Now why don't you hang up so my friend and I can say good-bye."

"Oh, sure. Nice talkin' ta ya, Angela's friend."

"Yeah, same here."

There was a loud click and silence. Angela waited a few seconds then asked, "You still there, Sharon?"

There was a giggle and another click.

Sounding exasperated, Katherine asked how often that happened.

Angela laughed. "Often enough to keep life interesting."

"Well, if that's true, it looks like the only way you and I will ever be able to have a private conversation is if I come up there."

"Yup. Prob'bly so."

"Oh, Angela. Please tell me you haven't gone country."

"Why? Would that be so bad?"

"That settles it. I'm coming up."

"When?"

"The sooner the better. Get that trailer ready."

10
THE SCHOOL

Monica raced toward the milking shed. "We're gonna have a school." She was so excited she stepped in a pile of nannyberries, lost her balance and landed flat on her rear.

"Watch yourself," chuckled Angela. "Bucky's been sniffing around."

"Now you tell me." Apparently undaunted by the accident, Monica stood up, brushed off the back of her jeans and joined Angela in the shed. "Is that Dolly?"

"Yes," replied Angela. "She's been acting really strange lately. Do you think something's wrong with her?" She finished milking the goat and moved a half-filled bucket off the stanchion.

Monica ran her hand along the goat's backbone. Puffs of dust drifted in the air. "Maybe she ate something that didn't agree with her. Have you noticed any unusual weeds in the pen?"

"There were some mayapples a couple of weeks back but I think I got rid of them."

"Why'd you do that?" shrieked Monica. "I could have transplanted them and made jelly from the fruit."

Angela raised her eyebrows and looked down her nose at Monica. "Wouldn't do that if I were you. Did you know some people call them Devil's Apples?"

"Oh, phish posh," snapped Monica. "That's just an old wives' tale."

"Well, old wives' tale or not, I wouldn't take any chances."

Angela carried the bucket to a nearby table, strained its contents into a large glass jug and covered the jug with a tight-fitting lid. "What's all this about a school?"

"Steve wants to run a week-long vacation bible school for all the kids in the hollow. He says we'll have bible stories, songs, games and maybe even puppet shows."

Even though Angela wanted to support Steve and Monica's efforts, she remembered what her friends had gone through trying to get people to attend their Sunday services. "That's pretty ambitious. Do you think many children will come?"

"Steve talked to Pam and Sharon and they both promised to make their kids come. That makes four. I thought maybe I'd go door to door and let everyone else in the area know about it."

Angela's eyes lit up. "I'll help."

A delighted grin spread across Monica's face. "Really?"

"Sure," replied Angela. "It'll be fun. Besides, I've been wanting to meet some of the other neighbors."

For the next four days, Angela and Monica drove up and down dirt roads, searched ridges and hidden passages, and knocked on doors trying to sell their idea. Most people they talked to were pleasant but few seemed excited about sending their children to summer school, let alone a summer bible school. One mother said her son was involved in 4-H; another that her children had to help with haying. Several people said they weren't even aware there was a new church in the hollow. By the end of the week, Angela and Monica had one *for sure,* three *maybes,* and ten *I don't knows.* Not willing to admit defeat, they convinced Steve to make an announcement at the Sunday service.

"I have exciting news," he began. "We're going to hold our first vacation bible school."

Attendance at the weekly service had picked up so that now there were about fifteen people sitting in the pews and a handful of men gathered around the door. Most of the women smiled enthusiastically but none of the men appeared overjoyed by Steve's announcement. "When's it gonna be, preacher?" asked a woman.

"Yeah — and what's it gonna cost?" sneered her husband.

The woman jabbed an elbow into her husband's ribs.

"It'll start in two weeks, right after the Fourth of July. And the best part is it's free."

A man wearing bib overalls and a faded yellow shirt lowered his head and sheepishly raised his hand. "Kin everyone go or jist the kids?"

Steve smiled. "Since this is our first time, we'll have to limit it to children. But that means all the children, not just the little ones."

"Do we gotta drive 'em ourselves or is you gonna pick 'em up?"

Monica joined her husband at the front of the church. "Either way," she said. "If you can get them to the road, we'll pick them up in our truck."

A tall woman with wrinkled skin and coal-black hair stood up. "You ain't gonna make 'em handle snakes, is ya?"

"Of course not," replied Steve. "We're just

going to sing songs and tell stories. And, depending on the weather, we might even go frog hunting."

Someone laughed. "Ya mean giggin'?"

Steve smirked. "Yes. Giggin'."

"You kin only do that at night," said one man.

"Not so," disagreed another. "My pappy and I always done it durin' the day."

Taking hold of Steve's hand, Monica smiled at the congregation. "We'll do whatever the children want to do. All we need to know right now is how many will be coming."

"Mine will," stated Pam.

"Mine too," boasted Sharon.

A buzz of agreement spread throughout the church but one woman in the back remained silent. Noticing her, Monica asked, "Will your children be coming, Mrs. Judd?"

"Cain't," muttered the woman. "Ain't got no shoes."

Monica nodded reassuringly. "That's okay. It's summer. I don't imagine many of the other children will be wearing shoes, either."

The woman's eyes glistened as she whispered, "Bless you."

With only two weeks to get everything

ready, Monica and Steve had their hands full. They had to pick out storybooks, decide which games to play and figure out what snacks to serve. They tried talking Gilberto into helping with the food, but he begged off saying, "Someone has to take care of the farm." Angela wanted to ask what was really going on, but she was afraid of what her husband might tell her. Over the years, she'd learned not to ask questions she didn't want answered.

When the first day of school finally arrived, Angela hurried to get ready. Even though it was early morning, the temperature was already approaching 80 degrees. She considered wearing shorts and a tank top but quickly abandoned the idea. "Nope," she told Gizmo. "This school is a church thing and it wouldn't do for me to show up with bare skin. Imagine how that would set the mothers off. I'll just have to find something else."

After slipping into jeans, t-shirt and a pair of open-toed sandals, she raced down the hill toward Steve and Monica's farm. As she approached their house, she let out a yell. "Come on you guys. Let's get this show on the road."

Monica and Steve were outside working on the truck. Steve's head was buried under

the hood and Monica was pushing something around in the bed. "We've been up
since the crack of dawn," shouted Monica.
"Where have you been?" She pointed at the
blankets and pillows surrounding her feet.
"Whaddaya think? Will this be comfortable
enough for the kids?"

Steve poked his head out from under the
hood and voiced his opinion. "Those kids
are used to getting tossed around in the
back of trucks. They won't know what to do
with pillows."

Monica picked up one of the pillows and
shook it at her husband. "Yeah, but I do."

He ducked back under the hood.

"What's wrong with the truck?" asked Angela.

"Nothing," grumbled Monica. "Mr.
Goodwrench here decided to check everything over before picking up the kids.
Something about not wanting anything to
go wrong while he was in charge of driving
them around. If he doesn't get cutting,
we're going to be late."

"I'm almost done," muttered Steve.

"How many children do we have to pick
up?" asked Angela.

"I'm not sure," replied Monica. "Pam said
she'd drive her kids and Sharon's to the
church. As for the others, I guess we'll have

to wait and see."

Steve slammed the hood shut, wiped his hands on a greasy shop towel and announced, "Okay — Let's do it." Monica and Angela jumped into the truck bed and off they went.

When they reached the first pick-up point, Steve stopped the truck, honked the horn and waited. No one showed. He honked the horn again. Still no one. He drove to the second and third stops but with the same results. Finally, at the fourth stop he found a small girl waiting along the roadside. In her hands was a bouquet of black-eyed Susans.

"Thought you forgot 'bout me," said the girl. Her thick red hair was coarse and wild looking but her smile was straight out of a *Fra Angelico* painting.

Monica jumped out of the truck and scooped the girl up in her arms. "Now how could we forget about you?" She hugged the girl and lifted her and her flowers up to Angela. "You're our most important student."

And maybe our only student, thought Angela.

The little girl's name was Florence. "Like that baudy-ville man." She seemed proud to be named after a famous man. "My momma's ma-maw used to be in baudy-ville but she never danced fer him . . . just fer carny shows. I never been to no carny show. Have you?"

Angela and Monica chatted with the girl while they bounced down the road. The girl said she was five and one-quarter years old, that she would be starting first grade in the fall, and that her pappy told her she probably wasn't going to like school. "Think that be true?" Angela hoped not.

As they neared the church, they heard singing.

"What's that?" asked Angela.

Monica brushed the hair from her eyes and smiled. "Sounds like our students."

Pam and Sharon watched from the doorway as Steve parked the truck in front of the church. "The children were restless," explained Pam. "So we started without you. Hope you don't mind."

Twelve mostly-shoeless children sat in a circle in the middle of the church singing the old Appalachian hymn, *Tell Me the Story of Jesus.* There were more girls than boys. Their alto voices laid the perfect backdrop for the boys' baritone harmony.

When the song ended, Monica and Steve walked to the front of the church and introduced themselves. "For anyone who doesn't know us, my name is Steve and this is my wife Monica."

"Don't we gotta call you 'Preacher' or sumpin?" asked one of the boys.

Steve laughed. "No, just call us Steve and Monica."

"But that ain't respectful," objected one of the girls. "How 'bout we call ya Mr. Steve and Mz. Monica?"

"That would be fine," said Monica. Motioning toward the back of the church, she added, "And this lady is Miss Angela."

"Gizmo's mom." The children cheered.

"Yes," agreed Steve, "Gizmo's mom. Now, let's all gather around, bow our heads and thank the Lord for giving us such a beautiful day."

After some shuffling of feet and muffled groaning, the children did as requested. Then, when the prayer was finished, Monica jumped into action. "Okay . . . everyone outside. We're going to start with a treasure hunt."

"Treasure hunt?" questioned one of the older boys. "Are we gonna look fer gold?"

"No, not gold, but something equally valuable." Steve laughed and led the way. Once outside he explained the game.

"Before you got here, Miss Monica and I hid some playing cards all around the outside of the church. Now, they aren't in any dangerous places like in the river or down groundhog holes, but they might be in a bucket, hanging from a tree or tied to a rock. All you have to do is find one, bring it to me and I'll give you a prize. As for rules, stay within my sight, big kids help the little ones, no pushing or shoving and don't take anyone else's card. You have ten minutes, starting now."

Screaming happily, the children scattered. Within seconds one of the boys returned bearing a nine-of-hearts. Right behind, little Florence ran up holding an ace.

"That was easy," said the boy. "Kin I go back an git'a nudder one?"

"No," scolded Monica. "Mr. Steve said only one per person."

"Ah, shucks." The boy launched a stream of brown gunk that splattered when it hit the ground.

"And there'll be no chawin' at this school." Monica pressed an empty coffee can against the boy's chin. "Give it up," she demanded.

The boy obeyed.

Ten minutes later, all of the children had returned. Steve gathered them together and instructed them to show him their cards. "Okay," he said, "we'll start with the lowest card and work our way up. Does anyone have a two?"

"Me," shouted a girl.

"Good. And what's your name?"

"Sally Ann Smithfield," replied the girl.

"Because you found the two, Sally, you have won a picture of Jesus."

The girl took the picture from Steve's hands and studied it. "I ain't never seen Jesus a'fore. Is this what he really looks like?"

"Maybe," replied Steve. "But it was so long ago, no one really knows. He could have looked like me or even like your father or one of your brothers."

"Not my brothers," disagreed the girl. "They're all ugly."

The other children laughed but Steve quickly hushed them. "Let's keep going . . . does anyone have a three?"

A boy rushed up and handed Steve his card. "This be a three, Mr. Steve?"

Steve looked at the card. "You're Tommy Brown, aren't you?"

"Yeth." The boy's almond shaped eyes sparkled with excitement. His face was round and his protruding tongue was thick.

"Well, Tommy. It looks like a three but it's actually an eight."

Several older boys snickered but Steve

ignored them. "I can see how you might think it was a three . . . they both have the same curviness. But that's all right, you still get a prize." He handed the boy a statue of Saint Nicholas. "Saint Nicholas is the patron saint of children."

"He's Sandy Craws, right?"

"Some people say so." Steve took his eyes off Tommy and stared at the boys who snickered. "You see, he used to travel around the country rewarding good children with presents and punishing those that were bad."

The chastised boys hung their heads as Steve continued calling numbers. When he got to the ace, Florence walked up and asked, "Am I next, preacher?"

"Yes, Florence, you are."

Steve handed the girl a small box. When she opened it, her mouth dropped open and her eyes grew large. "An angel." Florence traced the outline of the angel pin with her tiny finger. "She's so purty," she whispered.

Monica pinned the angel to Florence's t-shirt. "It's a guardian angel and it will help protect you. Do you like it?" asked Monica.

"Oh, yes," sighed the girl. "And you know what? I think I'm gonna like school, too."

Angela studied the children. Ranging in age from barely walking to mid-teens, they were dressed in old but clean clothes. Some even looked starched and pressed. How many times had those clothes been passed down and how many times had they been pressed? Were the children shoeless because it was summer or, like the woman in church confessed, because they didn't own shoes? Steve and Monica had experience working with children in third-world countries but what did she know? Sure, she had a couple college courses under her belt but none of them had anything to do with education or childcare. She'd never even raised a child.

She kicked a rock and watched as it rolled down the hill. At first, the rock moved slowly and almost deliberately between the weeds. But, the further it went, the faster it moved. Along the way, it hit other rocks and jarred them loose from their resting places. Suddenly, everything became clear. It didn't matter that she didn't have experience or teaching credentials. It didn't matter that she hadn't raised her own child. What mattered was that she had been given an opportunity to have an influence on these children's lives. Maybe even make a difference.

Was this the reason God sent her to West Virginia?

11
GIVING BACK

It was a quiet, sunlit morning and the only sounds were two hummingbirds racing back and forth in search of nectar. Angela sat on her front steps and counted her blessings. In less than two years, she had moved from smoggy Indiana to sunny Florida, made several warm, caring friends, learned to play bocce, gone on her first cruise and married a man who turned out to be the great love of her life. Then, just when she thought things couldn't get any better, she moved to West Virginia and began living the happy and healthy life she'd always wanted. She was getting more fresh air and exercise than she had in years, she and Monica grew their own vegetables and milked their own goats, and the church that Steve started had become an integral part of her life — especially the bible school.

Every day at the school was amazing. One morning she spent an hour talking to two ill-tempered brothers about Cain and Abel, the next she showed a brace-legged girl how to catch butterflies. Before lunch, she stood guard as everyone washed their hands and said grace before eating. In the afternoon, she read to the children from books Steve received from a generous patron. At the end of each school day, she hugged the girls and playfully patted the boys on the back as they were leaving. None of the children objected. In fact, most of them either laughed or hugged back. But bible school only lasted one week. What was she going to do when it was over?

On the final day of school, little Florence came up with an answer. "Miss Angela, I ain't got nuttin' to do fer the rest'a the summer. Kin I come over and help ya take care'a Gizmo?"

Inspired by Florence, another girl volunteered her services. "I could brush the goats." Then, straightening his shoulders, a serious-looking young boy stepped forward. "I'd be proud ta tend your garden." His broad smile revealed two missing front teeth.

That was it. If the children spent their free time helping out around the farm, she could keep working with them. Of course, she wasn't a certified teacher or anything near it so she'd have to call their time together something other than school. Maybe she could just say it was a meeting. Or camp. Yes, that was it . . . camp. But what should she name it? She'd call Katherine. Maybe she could come up with something catchy.

Surprisingly, Katherine was no help. "What do I know about kids?" She sounded like a cat with its nose caught in a mousetrap. "I stay as far away from rug rats as possible."

Getting similar responses from everyone she talked to, Angela finally settled on the name *Camp Gizmo*. After all, if it wasn't for that absurd landlord saying she had to get rid of her dog, she might have been stuck in Indiana for the rest of her life. Just thinking about it gave her goose bumps.

The children loved the name and, true to their word, worked hard to make Camp Gizmo a success. Even though they all had chores to do at home, they managed to find enough time to work with Angela. Every morning around nine, six or seven kids armed with bag lunches and a variety of weathered garden tools showed up at Steve and Monica's farm. Ready for whatever work Angela chose for them that day, they wore shorts, tank tops and, for the most part, no shoes. They never grumbled about the work being too hard or the weather being too hot. They never said they were too tired or too busy. They never asked if they were going to be paid.

Pam's boys borrowed their father's mower, cut the overgrown pastures and raked the downed grass into windrows. The older boy offered free advice. "Next year we'll need to do this earlier. Like in May. The early cutting be more nutritious fer the animals." Three days later, they came back with balers and compressed the dried grass into rectangular bundles that they loaded onto a flatbed truck and carried to the pole barn.

Not to be outdone by the boys, several of the girls took over goat patrol. They made sure the goat pen was kept clear of unwanted critters, they did the daily grooming and they even jerry-rigged some leashes and collars so they could walk the goats. "Them goats'll be needing shots a'fore kidding season," one girl advised. "I kin do it for ya. My sister's boyfriend works in a drugstore. He showed me how." About the only thing the children didn't do was the milking. That was a job Monica and Angela preferred to keep for themselves.

In addition to helping with Gizmo, Florence and some of the smaller children worked in the garden. Using the tools they brought from home, they crawled around on their hands and knees, pulled weeds by the bushel-load and turned the soil until it was as fine as cornmeal. They even put chicken wire around the corn and tomatoes hoping it would ward off some of the groundhogs and terrapins.

One of the boys had a huge silver boom box he kept tuned to the local country music station. Cranking up the volume, the kids kept right on working while they stomped their feet and sang along with Reba, Willy and the Statlers. It was like a great big hoedown and, even though she wasn't especially fond of country music, Angela was thrilled to be a part of it.

As they worked side by side, the children joked with Angela and asked all sorts of questions. One girl wanted to know if it was okay for twelve-year-olds to date. Angela advised her not to rush into anything. Another asked her about school. "There's this girl at my school, she's black and some'a the other kids say to stay away from her cuz she's bad. But I like her. What should I do?"

Even though Angela had run into prejudice before, she was a little surprised it had reared its ugly head in the backwoods hollows. Their very seclusion made her think the hollows were shielded from some of life's baser aspects. Maybe she was wrong.

Knowing whatever she said could have a huge effect on the girl's life, Angela measured her words carefully. "The color of a person's skin doesn't make them good or bad. It's what they do — how they act and how they treat other people. Has this girl ever hit you?"

"No," replied the girl.

"Does she use bad words?"

"No."

"Then give her a chance. Get to know her. Spend time with her and then decide for yourself whether she is good or bad."

The girl sighed and looked away from Angela. "What if the other kids tease me?"

"There's an old saying about sticks and stones . . ."

"Yeah, I know," groaned the girl. "Sticks and stones may break my bones but words will never hurt me. That's what my maw always tells me."

Angela ruffled the girl's hair. "And don't you forget it."

The work the children did was yielding remarkable results. The goats were producing more milk, Gizmo seemed livelier than he had been in years, and whether it was all the herbs and marigolds the children planted or the garlic and pepper juice they sprayed, the garden was producing more than anyone expected. There were two-pound tomatoes, foot-long zucchinis, and enough corn, beans, carrots and potatoes to frighten a Crock-Pot. Angela taught Monica how to use a pressure canner and Gilberto offered up his favorite potato bread recipe. But, even though they shared some of the bumper crop with neighbors, Angela worried that the leftovers might be wasted.

"We could take 'em to the farmers' market," suggested one of Sharon's girls.

"Yeah, and maybe some goat cheese and bread, too," said the other.

Angela slapped her forehead. "Gee, why didn't I think of that?"

Back in Indiana, Angela and her brother ran a vegetable stand every summer when they were kids. Working from a small shed their father built out by the road, they sold homegrown tomatoes in the summer and Jack O'Lantern pumpkins in the fall. Sometimes they even ventured out into the countryside and collected wild raspberries, pawpaw fruits and hickory nuts. They didn't make a lot of money but with the milk from Angela's 4-H Guernsey and the eggs they collected from their chickens, they never went hungry.

For the next couple of days, Angela, Monica, Steve and the children prepared for the farmers' market. Monica called the co-op to find out if they needed a license to sell produce. Steve built a sunshade to protect the tender veggies. Angela collected boxes, bushels and burlap bags to transport everything. And the children created signs to hang all over town. Everyone but Gilberto got involved. One week after coming up with the idea, everything was ready.

The first day of market, scores of townspeople poured out of their shops and offices and headed for the Lutheran church parking lot. There were bankers and doctors, mechanics and store clerks. Some were in suits; others were in overalls and rubber boots. Five or six farmers were selling their produce from the backs of their trucks but everyone seemed interested in what the children had to offer.

A haughty-looking woman dressed in designer jeans and a green silk blouse walked up to Angela and demanded a sample of the goat cheese. "After all, I don't want to buy a pig in a poke, now do I?" Her voice was high-pitched and annoying.

Biting her tongue, Angela took the lid off a plastic container, scooped a small amount of cheese onto a plastic spoon and handed it to the woman. At first, the woman just swirled the cheese around on her tongue. Then, announcing it was the best cheese she had ever tasted, she bought every available container plus two loaves of Gilberto's potato bread.

The owner of the sandwich shop bought all the tomatoes and half of the corn, while two ladies from the dress shop argued over the rest. Business was so good everything was sold before noon.

As the children packed up to leave, an elderly woman approached. "I wasn't able to plant a garden this year." She almost seemed apologetic. "Do you think you could come back tomorrow and bring me a bushel of tomatoes? I do so love canned tomatoes."

The children turned toward Angela who grinned, nodded and replied, "Absolutely."

From then on, Angela and the children from Camp Gizmo went to the farmers' market every Friday and Saturday. They sold vegetables from their own and their parents' gardens, made-from-scratch breads and muffins, homemade jams and jellies, and three different varieties of goat cheese. In less than two months, they earned just over seven hundred dollars, all of which was sitting in a bank account collecting interest.

On closing day of the market, Steve asked

the children what they were going to do with the money.

Bobby Ray Talbot, the serious-looking boy who months earlier offered, "ta tend your garden," spoke up first. "We bin talking and decided we'd like ta buy a bell fer the church. The ol' one got stole about five year ago and no one could ever find it. If we got a new 'un, we could ring it of a Sunday mornin' and everyone would know it was time fer meeting."

"Yeah," bellowed another boy. "Gotta know when it's time fer meeting."

"Well, that's very generous," said Steve. "But wouldn't you rather spend the money on something for yourselves?"

The boys signaled for the others to join them and they all scrunched down in a huddle. After a few minutes of heated discussion and wild hand gestures, a decision was made.

Bobby Ray, the obvious spokesman of the group, delivered the verdict. "Yup, we all want the bell. My paw checked on the internet where he works and found a place we kin buy one. It ain't brass or gold or anything but it's big enough to fill that ol' bell tower. We might hafta put up some new boards and such but that shouldn't be no problem. Paw says all we gotta do is send off a certified check and they'll ship that bell direct to the church. No extree charge. 'Course, if there be any money left, maybe we could use it for the Harvest Festival."

"That's right," exclaimed Steve. "Harvest Festival is less than two weeks off."

"Oh my gosh." Angela heaved a sigh and shook her head. "That means Katherine is coming. I'd nearly forgotten."

"Is that going to be a problem?" asked Monica.

"Well, no. It's just that I've got a lot of things to do before she gets here."

Monica frowned. "Like what?"

Using her fingers to keep track of the chores, Angela rattled off her list. "For starters, I've got to get the trailer ready. Then I've got to clean the house and go grocery shopping, and of course . . ."

"We'll help," shouted the children.

"Oh, no," protested Angela. "You kids have done so much already, I couldn't possibly ask you to do any more. Besides, you've got to get ready for school."

One of the older boys raised his voice. "School don't start till after Labor Day and since there ain't much growin' in the garden right now, we got nuttin' else to do."

"Yeah, that's right," agreed the others.

Monica leaned toward Angela and whispered in her ear. "Maybe we should use the time to teach them English."

Angela laughed and playfully pushed Monica away. "Well, okay. As long as your parents don't mind, I'd appreciate your help. But first things first. Bobby Ray, talk to your dad and find out how much the bell will cost. Then, Monday morning, let's all get together, come back into town and get that certified check. After that, we'll split up whatever is left and get some ice cream. Agreed?"

"Hurray." The children cheered and hugged one another.

The following Monday, all the kids piled into Steve's truck and headed for town. Because Monica stayed home to take care of the goats, Angela sat in the front seat with Steve. Along the way, she thought she saw Gilberto's truck headed in the opposite direction but she wasn't sure because it was going so fast and so many other trucks looked just like his. Besides, there was a woman in the passenger seat and it was doubtful Gil would be driving around with anyone, let alone a woman. After all, how many people did he know in town?

When they reached the bank, Steve, Angela and the group of kids went inside and informed the bank clerk that they wanted a certified check "in the amount of five hundred, twenty-seven dollars and ninety-two cents." Explaining that he would have to get the bank president's approval, the amused clerk excused himself and disappeared into a closed office. Ten minutes later, he reappeared with check in hand. The children then informed him that they wanted to close out their account and, "would you give it to us in cash, please?"

While Steve divvied up the remaining cash, Angela filled in the name on the check, placed it in an envelope and dropped it in a mailbox. "Now, let's get that ice cream," she ordered.

The children ran across the street to the corner diner. When Steve and Angela arrived, they noticed Gilberto's truck. "Hey, that's Gil's truck, isn't it?" Steve sounded surprised.

Angela checked the license plate. "Yes, it is."

"That's great. Did you tell him to meet us here?"

"No, I didn't." Angela's stomach flipped like a pancake. When she reached the diner door, she opened it and looked inside. Gilberto was sitting at a table with Gelah. They were holding hands.

A cold chill crawled up Angela's back and

her ears began to buzz. She felt her head go light. And then the world went black.

12
THE HOSPITAL

Angela didn't know what she was looking at. It was white and bumpy and there were two round things that looked like dirty snowballs. As her eyes focused, she realized the snowballs were light bulbs and the bumps were the pattern on a painted tin ceiling. A hairy black spider was working its way across the ceiling. *What happened,* she wondered. *Why am I lying on the floor?*

Gilberto was at her side. "Lie still, Angela. You have fainted and the ambulance is on its way."

"Ambulance? I don't need an ambulance."

She tried to get up but Gilberto gently pushed her shoulders to the floor. Looking beyond his worried face, she saw those of Steve and the children. "Don't worry, kids. I'm okay."

Little Florence threw herself on Angela's body and burst into tears. "Please don't die, Miss Angela. I love you."

"I'm not going to die, Florence. I fainted because I forgot to eat breakfast this morning."

"We will let the doctor decide that," Gilberto's tone was anxious but firm. She was too bewildered to argue.

The sudden blare of a siren confirmed the ambulance's approach. Within seconds, two male EMTs carrying a stretcher, oxygen tank, and a large black box rushed through the diner door. "All right, everyone, give us room."

One of the men knelt beside Angela and asked if she remembered what happened. She noticed his eyes were iridescent-green and his arms well developed. Resisting the urge to reach out and touch his muscles, she told him what little she knew.

"I walked in and, next thing, I was on the floor."

"Have you ever had an episode like this before?" asked the technician.

"No." Had she really seen what she thought she saw?

"Do you have heart trouble?"

"No." Maybe it was just her imagination.

"Do you take any medications?"

"No." Maybe it wasn't.

"Okay. Let's check you over and then we'll be ready to go."

Angela snapped back to reality. "Go? Go where?"

"We're going to take you to the hospital."

Panic took over. "I don't like hospitals. Can't I just go see a doctor tomorrow?"

"I'm afraid not, mam. Procedure demands we take all elderly fainting victims to the hospital for evaluation."

Elderly? Did he just say elderly?

Realizing the young man wasn't going to back down, Angela allowed him to check her pulse and attach a blood pressure cuff to her arm. Next, he listened to her heart. Was it still beating?

Having determined she was stable enough to transport, the young man instructed the other EMT to bring the gurney over. Gently lifting her, they placed Angela on the stretcher and rushed her to the ambulance. Gilberto followed in his truck.

When they reached the hospital, Gilberto ran to Angela's side as the EMTs wheeled her into an emergency room cubicle. "Everything will be all right, *amore mio*. You will see."

She wasn't so sure. She had just witnessed her husband holding hands with another woman. *Why?* They hadn't even been married a year. Was he already tired of her? She closed her eyes and didn't respond to

Gilberto. Right then, she wished he wasn't even there.

Angela was still lying on the gurney when a white-smocked doctor entered the examination area and introduced himself.

"I am Dr. Abdul Malik. And you are . . . ?" His name was foreign but he spoke perfect English.

"Angela. Angela Fontero."

The doctor smiled as he turned toward Gilberto. "And you, sir?"

"I am her husband, Gilberto Fontero."

"Well, it is very nice to meet you, Mr. Fontero. But would you mind waiting outside while I talk to your wife?"

"Oh, of course." Gilberto nodded his head and reluctantly backed out of the cubicle.

"The EMTs tell me you fainted at the diner," said the doctor. "Was the food that bad?"

Doctor Malik was dark skinned, black-haired and short. His chocolate-brown eyes were gentle and his attempt at humor comforting.

"I guess I forgot to eat," replied Angela.

"Ahh. That'll do it." The doctor loosened the top button of Angela's blouse and placed a stethoscope on her chest. "When was the last time you had an EKG?"

"Why? Is something wrong?"

"No." He removed the stethoscope and motioned for Angela to sit up. "Your heart sounds strong but it is still racing. In itself, fainting isn't serious but I want to make sure there isn't some underlying reason. I would like to do an ultrasound and maybe a few other tests."

"Can we do the tests in your office?" Angela wanted to get out of there as soon as possible and go . . . where? Home? Steve and Monica's? She wished Katherine were there so she could cry on her shoulder.

"I don't have the proper equipment in my office. I'm afraid we'll have to do the tests here. Have you had your yearly physical yet?"

Rather than admit she hadn't had a checkup in more than ten years, Angela shook her head.

As if knowing her secret, the doctor smiled. "That's fine. As long as you're here, we'll do a complete workup just to make sure everything is in working order. We'll start with the ultrasound and some blood tests and then go from there."

"How long will all that take?"

"Probably no more than two days."

"Two days?" She looked around the room for a way to escape.

"Don't worry," said the doctor. "We have

cable TV. When was the last time you watched cable?"

Angela snickered and shook her head. "Quite a while. We live back in the hollows and only get three stations. Two if it's raining."

"Well then, you're in for a treat."

A nurse steered a wheelchair into the examination area. "Let's get you checked in, Mrs. Fontero."

"I can walk," objected Angela.

"Sorry," replied the nurse, "the insurance company insists."

Gilberto jumped from his chair in the waiting room when he saw the nurse wheel Angela out of the emergency room. "What did the doctor say? Are you all right?" He reached for Angela's hand but she buried it under the sheet covering her knees.

"I'm fine but they want to keep me for a couple of days. I didn't bring my purse with me this morning. Do you have your insurance card?"

Obviously stunned by Angela's frosty behavior, Gilberto backed away from the wheelchair. "Sí," he replied forlornly. "I will take care of the paperwork. Then I will come up to your room to make sure you are settled in properly."

Angela shrugged her shoulders. "That's

really not necessary, Gil. But maybe you'd like to run out to Pawpaw to make sure Gelah got home safely." She gestured for the nurse to move on.

After the nurse took her to a room and left her alone, Angela laced her fingers on the back of her neck and broke into tears. "Why is this happening? Am I such a bad person that God has to punish me?"

"You are *not* a bad person, Angela." Monica appeared out of nowhere and cradled the sobbing Angela in her arms. "You've just had some bad things happen. Now go ahead and cry your eyes out. You deserve it."

Angela did as instructed. When her tears finally ran out, she thanked Monica. "How did you know I was here?"

"Steve called me from town."

"What did he say?" Angela wasn't really sure she wanted to know.

"Just that you were taken to the hospital and needed a friend."

"Did he tell you about Gil and Gelah?"

"Yes, but I wouldn't worry about that."

"I catch my husband holding hands with another woman and you tell me not to worry?" Angela's tears dried into rage.

"Calm down, Angela. I'm sure there's a good explanation."

"Like what? That he likes older women?"

"You know, things aren't always what they seem, Angela. Maybe he has a good explanation."

"Can we talk about something else?" Angela broke away from Monica and walked to the window. Outside, Gilberto was standing in the parking lot looking up. She took two steps back.

"Of course. Any idea how long they're gonna keep you here?"

"The doctor said two days."

"I thought you only fainted." Monica sat on the edge of the bed and bounced. Her frown indicated it was hard.

"I did but he wants to run all kinds of tests. You know how doctors are. Once they get their hands on you, they don't let go."

"Maybe so, but a couple days away from the farm might do you a lot of good."

A look of concern crossed Angela's face. "Oh my gosh. What about the children? Are they all right?"

"Steve drove them home right after he called me. I'm sure they're fine."

"What about the goats? And Gizmo? I've got to get home and take care of them."

Monica glared at Angela. "Will you quit worrying? I'll take care of the goats and Steve will take care of your mangy dog. Now what about you? What do you need? Pajamas? Magazines? What?"

"Thanks, Monica, but don't bother. I'll be okay."

"It's not a bother," said Monica. "Tomorrow is my normal shopping day. I can milk the goats in the morning, run into town, stop by here, do the shopping and still be home in time for the evening milking."

"Well, if you're sure you were coming into town anyway."

Monica crossed her legs. "I'm sure."

"Then can I ask a small favor?"

"Sure. What?"

"Could you pick up some chocolate when you get the magazines?"

"Anything your heart desires."

Monica jumped off the bed when a teenaged candy striper marched into the room and announced she needed to take Angela downstairs for the ultrasound. Hightailing it for the door, she only stopped long enough to kiss Angela's cheek. "I'll see you in the morning." Her voice was cheerful and full of promise. "Now get some rest and don't worry, everything is gonna work out."

As she pushed Angela's wheelchair down the hall, the candy striper launched into her life history. "My name is Bobby Jo Phillips and I just started working here. In fact, you're my first ultrasound patient. I never had an ultrasound. Does it hurt?"

Angela smiled and said, "I hope not."

The hospital was only three stories but the lab was in the basement so they had to take an elevator to reach it. The girl parked Angela's wheelchair in front of the elevator doors and pressed the down button. "My brother, Jimmy, wants to be a doctor some day. Right now, he's in the Army and pretty soon he'll be furloughed somewhere but we don't know where yet. Do you have any brothers or sisters?"

"Yes," replied Angela. "I have an older brother named Tony."

"Does he live in West Virginia?"

"No. He and his wife live in Florida."

The elevator arrived and Bobby Jo pushed Angela inside. "Oh, cool," she said. "My mom says she'll take me to Florida if I stay in school and graduate. My brother never did. He just quit and went into the Army. That made my mom really mad because she and my dad never finished either. That's why she promised me the trip."

"Well, school is very important," said Angela. "Do you know what kind of work you'd like to do after you graduate?"

"Gee, nobody's ever asked me that before. I dunno. I like animals. Maybe I could go to work at an animal hospital or something."

The elevator doors opened into the basement where several sets of swinging doors blocked entry into darkened rooms. The teenager studied the labels on each set of doors, and turned the wheelchair toward the one marked *Radiology.* After depositing Angela inside, she thanked her for the nice talk and left.

Angela looked around. The room was unadorned and cold. She hoped the ultrasound machine wouldn't be metal.

After what seemed like an hour, a skinny technician in green scrubs appeared. "My name is Rudy and I'll be performing a carotid ultrasound today."

"What's that?" asked Angela.

The technician pushed Angela's wheelchair through a wide door into a small room where an examination table and large white computer screen stood. "It's a test that determines whether the major arteries in the neck are blocked." Without making eye contact, he motioned toward the table. "Get on the table and lie face up. I am going to apply warm gel and maneuver a transducer across your neck and chest in order to capture the desired images. Hold very still during the procedure and no talking. When I am finished, someone will take you down the hall to draw blood." Rudy's manner dropped the room temperature an additional five degrees.

After rubbing gel on Angela's chest and neck, the technician told her to take a big breath and "let it out."

Angela tried to think of something else. *If it weren't for Gilberto, I'd be home with my dog and goats. Darn, I forgot to tell Monica how much food to feed Gizmo.*

Five minutes later, the test was over and she was back in the wheelchair. "Did you find anything unusual?" she asked.

"The doctor will go over the results with you later." The technician pushed Angela's wheelchair into the hallway and walked away.

Gee, nice bedside manner.

She started to feel chilled and rubbed her arms hoping to generate some heat. It didn't help. *I could freeze down here and no one would ever know. Not even Gil. That would serve him right.*

The elevator doors opened and Bobby Jo rushed out. "I am so sorry," she apologized. "I should have given you this before we left your room." She wrapped a blanket around Angela's trembling shoulders and arms.

Angela immediately felt better. "Thank you so much, Bobby Jo. I was beginning to feel like an ice cube. Why is it so cold down here, anyway?"

"The air conditioning is old," explained the teenager. "They turn it way up to keep the top floor cool. Of course, since cold settles, the basement gets super cold. That's why we always give people blankets before we bring them down here. Sorry, I forgot."

"Don't worry about it," replied Angela. "Are you going to take me to the blood lab?"

"Yes, and then I'll take you back upstairs. You were gone when they came by with the dinner menus so I filled one out for you. Hope you don't mind.

"Of course not." Angela hadn't eaten since breakfast. The thought of food made her mouth water. "What did you order?"

"Fried chicken, mashed potatoes, broccoli and apple crisp for dessert. Is that okay?"

"Perfect."

Following the blood test, Bobby Jo returned Angela to her room. Within minutes, an orderly brought in her dinner. Even though the fried chicken was dry and the broccoli overcooked, the mashed potatoes and apple crisp filled her stomach. When the potatoes started tasting like cold wood pulp, she pushed the tray table away, settled back on the bed and turned on the television. The emergency room doctor was right — the hospital had cable. She surfed through the available channels and settled on an *Animal Planet* program about meerkats. Five minutes into the show, a doctor entered her room.

"I am Doctor Jonas." The woman offered her hand to Angela. "I have reviewed your ultrasound and your heart and arteries look fine but I am a little concerned about a shadow in your breast."

"My breast? I thought that guy was taking pictures of my heart."

"Actually, it was everything from your neck down to your waist."

"So, what's wrong with my breast?"

"It looks like you may have a cyst."

"Is that bad?"

"Usually not, but I'd like to do another test tomorrow just to be sure."

"What kind of test?"

"It's called an FNAB or fine needle aspiration biopsy. I'll insert a hollow needle into the cyst, suck up some fluid and send it to pathology for testing. That way, we'll know what we're dealing with."

"If you don't mind my asking, what kind of doctor are you."

"I'm an oncologist."

13
BRACING FOR THE TRUTH

Angela tried to concentrate on the program dancing across the television screen but one word kept drumming in her brain. Cancer. Did the doctor just tell her she had *cancer?*

She reached for the telephone but quickly pulled her hand back. What good would it do to call anyone now? The doctor said there *might* be a cyst, not that there *was* one. And even if there was one, there was no guarantee it was malignant. Why get everyone all worked up over a silly *what-if.* But what about Gil? Didn't he have a right to know what was going on? No, she thought. Not after the way he'd been acting.

She got out of the bed and walked to the window. It was only August but signs of autumn were already visible. Across the parking lot, leaves littered the ground beneath the few straggly trees. A v-shaped flock of birds — *Canada geese?* — raced across the horizon. A woman walking out of the hospital buttoned her sweater. It was getting dark earlier. In a few months, there would be snow. Where was she going to be when winter arrived? At home making Christmas cookies or in the hospital undergoing chemo?

A nurse entered the room and asked Angela if she wanted a sleeping pill. Her first inclination was to decline but, considering the events of the day, she gave in. "Sure, why not."

Swallowing the pill, she crawled back into bed. The meerkats were gone and now an able-looking young man was wrestling a toothy alligator. How did someone learn to do that? Why would they even want to? Her eyes grew heavy and she drifted into sleep as the man and alligator battled it out.

Her ex-husband Carl, and her present husband Gilberto, were chasing Gizmo down a white sand beach. Carl was wearing a cowboy hat and Gilberto was carrying a doily. The sun was shining but there were thick, dark clouds in the sky.

Down the beach, a skinny green man walking an alligator on a leash stepped into a groundhog hole. He fell to his knees and lost control of the reptile. The alligator whipped its head around and, spotting

Gizmo, headed in the dog's direction. Carl and Gilberto saw the alligator coming but nonchalantly moved off in the opposite direction. The green man picked himself up, shrugged his shoulders and skipped after them.

Angela screamed but no sound came out. She started running.

Gizmo stood his ground as the menacing alligator approached. He didn't bark but every muscle in his body tensed.

Out of nowhere, Bucky the goat appeared standing in the middle of a wooden plank teeter-totter. Gizmo joined him and together they waited.

When the alligator got close enough to snap at Gizmo, the dog walked toward the middle forcing his end of the plank high into the air. When the alligator ran toward the lowered end, Gizmo backed up and Bucky walked toward the middle. Each time the alligator snapped, the dog and goat were able to avoid its razor-sharp teeth.

The sand turned to mud and Angela was crawling up a hill toward the ridge. Giant iridescent bugs crawled everywhere. The bugs tried to bite her but she fought them off with a paintbrush. She heard someone singing. It sounded like children. Up the hill, she could see the alligator's tail but every time she reached out to grab it, she slipped in the mud and slid backwards. Gizmo and Bucky called to her but she kept sliding down, down, down the hill.

"Mrs. Fontero?" The green man was shaking her arm. "It's time to wake up."

Angela opened her eyes. It wasn't the green man — it was an orderly. "I'm going to take you down to the first floor for your surgery."

"Surgery? What surgery? I thought I was only having a test." Had she slept through the whole thing?

The orderly positioned a wheelchair next to Angela's bed. "Your chart says they're performing an FNAB. That's sort of like surgery, isn't it?"

"I hope not." Angela slipped a pair of hospital-supplied slippers on her feet and got into the wheelchair. She thought about calling Gilberto but there wasn't time.

Dr. Jonas was waiting as the orderly wheeled Angela into the operating room. "We could have done this in your room," explained the doctor, "but I prefer the lighting in here."

"Are you going to do a test or some kind of surgery?" On the way down, Angela made her mind up to walk out of the hospital if the doctor even mentioned surgery.

"Don't worry, Angela, it's just a test." The doctor smiled and patted the paper-covered operating table. "Can you hop up or do you need help?"

"I can do it." She pushed the wheelchair aside and sat on the edge of the table. "Should I lie down?"

"No," replied the doctor. "Not just yet."

The doctor flipped a switch and the room came alive with light. It dawned on Angela that this room had been chosen so the doctor could see what she was doing. That, thought Angela, was a good thing.

After moving a portable ultrasound machine next to the operating table, Dr. Jonas loosened the left shoulder of Angela's gown and placed a folded blanket over her exposed breast. "The first thing I'll do," said the doctor, "is wash your skin with an antiseptic. Then I'll give you a shot so you won't feel anything while I'm doing the biopsy."

Angela pointed her nose toward the ultrasound machine. "What's that for?"

"The ultrasound will pinpoint the location of the cyst and the computer will help me guide the needle to it."

"Is this going to hurt?"

"Not a bit. Now just relax. It will all be over before you know it."

The doctor elevated the head of the operating table and signaled for Angela to lean back. She then applied the antiseptic, gave Angela a numbing shot and repositioned the ultrasound machine so she could view the computer monitor. "It will take a moment for the shot to take effect. Are you comfortable?"

"Yes. Thank you." Even though she felt half-naked, Angela was surprisingly comfortable. Thankfully, the room wasn't as cold as the one the night before and she barely felt the shot. The only thing bothering her was that bizarre dream. What did it mean and what caused it? Was it the dried-out chicken or the sleeping pill? If she had to stay in the hospital another night, she would skip both.

Using an instrument similar to the one the radiologist used, Dr. Jonas located the suspected cyst. "There it is," she announced. "Would you like to watch?"

Angela turned her head and stared at the ceiling. "No way. I'll pass, thank you." As forewarned, she felt some pressure and a slight pinching sensation. She moaned and took a deep breath.

"You're doing great," said the doctor, "just a few more pinpricks and we'll be done."

"You're going to do more than one?"

"Yes," replied the doctor. "I have to insert the needles several times to insure enough samples are taken."

"Then what happens?"

"The samples are sent to the pathologist who puts them under a microscope and examines them."

"How long before you get the results?"

"Depending on how many other samples he has to look at, we should know something in a couple of hours — this afternoon at the latest." The doctor placed a small bandage over the incision. "In the meantime, you can go back to your room and watch television."

"That's it? We're done?"

The doctor laughed. "Now that wasn't so bad, was it?" She walked Angela to a waiting area and told her someone would take her back to her room shortly. "I'll come see you as soon as I hear from the pathologist."

Angela liked the doctor. She seemed knowledgeable and explained things in uncomplicated terms. She had a positive attitude and she was kindhearted. Qualities like that made Angela believe everything was going to work out. Everything was going to be all right.

It was going on nine-o'clock when Angela got back to her room. Knowing Monica

186

wouldn't arrive for at least another hour, she decided to call Gilberto. Even though she was still angry, he needed to know about the biopsy and she needed a little TLC. All things considered, it was the least he could do.

Her hand shook as she dialed the number. What should she say? One short ring, two long rings. It was strange listening to the party-line signal. Was this the first time she'd called her own number? One ring, two rings again. No answer. One ring, two rings. Still no answer. Just when she was about to give up, someone picked up.

"Fontero residence."

"Steve? Is that you?"

"Angela." The preacher sounded like he'd been running. "How are you feeling?"

"I'm fine." She wondered why he was answering her phone. "Is Gil there?"

"No. When I came by to feed Gizmo, he was already gone. I thought he went to the hospital. Isn't he with you?"

"I haven't seen him but I've been out of my room for a while. Maybe he's around somewhere."

Steve chuckled. "Yeah. Knowing him, he's probably down in the kitchen showing the staff how to cook your food."

"I hope so," sighed Angela. "What I've

had so far isn't worth writing home about."

"Well, hang in there, Angela. And when Monica gets there please ask her to call me. She wanted me to do the laundry while she was gone but I don't remember how much soap she said to use."

"Sure Steve, I'll tell her to call." Angela hung up the phone and leaned back against the bed. She closed her eyes and tried to collect her thoughts. So much had happened so fast. She needed time to process everything. A soft knock invaded her thoughts.

"May I come in?" Gilberto stood in the doorway holding a small bouquet of roses. He was wearing the same clothes he'd worn the day before, only now they looked wrinkled. A coffee stain marred his otherwise white polo shirt. He hadn't shaved and it looked like he hadn't slept.

"I just called the house and spoke to Steve," barked Angela. "He said he hadn't seen you. Where have you been?"

"Here." Gilberto placed the flowers on Angela's bed and lowered his bloodshot eyes. "All night."

"You slept here?" She wondered if she was being too hard on him.

"Yes. In the waiting room."

Her tone softened. "Why?"

"I wanted to be nearby . . . in case you needed me."

There he was. The man she trusted, the man who made her feel safe, the man she fell in love with. Did he still love her? Did she still love him? She took a deep breath and asked the big question. "What's going on, Gil? Have you been seeing someone else?"

The color drained from Gilberto's face. "No, *amore mio*. How can you think that?"

"Here lately it's the only thing I've been able to think about. You don't seem interested in the farm anymore, you're spending a lot of time away and every time I ask if you want to do something, you say you have other plans." She held her breath and fixed her tear-filled eyes on the window. "I even dreamt about it last night."

"Was it a bad dream?"

"Yes. At first I didn't know what it all meant but now I've figured it out."

"Tell me about it."

"It was about protecting the ones you love. Gizmo was being chased by an alligator and Bucky came to his rescue."

"That must have frightened you."

"Yes, but the worst part was that you and my ex-husband were both in the dream and neither one of you tried to help him."

"I would never let any harm come to Gizmo."

"Well, that's what I used to think but you were carrying a doily."

"A doily?"

"Yes. And Carl was wearing a cowboy hat."

Gilberto frowned and shook his head in confusion.

"Carl ran off with a woman wearing a cowboy hat and Gelah makes doilies. I saw you holding hands with her yesterday and I put two and two together."

Gilberto hung his head. "Is that what caused you to faint?"

Angela shrugged her shoulders. "I'm not sure. The doctors are running a lot of tests. They found a cyst yesterday and did a biopsy this morning."

"A cyst?" Gilberto steadied himself against Angela's bed. "Where?"

"In my breast. But don't worry, it's probably nothing."

Gilberto reached for Angela's hand. "I should have known. I should have known."

"Should have known what?" Monica waltzed into the room carrying a small duffle bag, several magazines and a box of chocolates. She set the bag and magazines on a chair and placed the chocolates on

Angela's tray table.

"It's nothing," insisted Angela. "They did an ultrasound yesterday and found something suspicious in my breast so they performed a biopsy this morning."

Monica pushed her way between Angela and Gilberto. "A lump?"

"They said it might be a cyst." Angela reached for the box of chocolates and started to remove the lid.

"Stop that." Monica slapped Angela's hand. "Do they think it's cancer?"

"They won't know until the test results come back."

"And when will that be?" Monica had taken charge of the conversation. Gilberto was noticeably silent.

"Probably this afternoon." Angela pouted and cautiously reached for the chocolates. "I missed breakfast this morning. Can't I have just one?"

Gilberto handed the box to Angela. "As many as you desire, *amore mio*." Standing tall and directing his attention to Monica, he asserted his husbandly rights. "Angela and I have much to discuss, Monica. We would like to have some time alone."

"Oh. Sure. Of course." Monica raised her hands and backed toward the door. "I need to get to the grocery store anyway. Call me if you need anything, Angela. And Gil? we'll probably see you later. Right?"

Without taking his eyes off Angela, Gilberto nodded. "*Sì*. Later."

As soon as Monica was gone, Angela tore into Gilberto. "That was rude. How could you treat Monica like that?"

"Our life together is at stake," replied Gilberto. "Nothing is more important than that."

"You obviously didn't think so yesterday." Angela shoved the tray table aside so she could get out of bed. The box of chocolates went flying and pieces of candy rolled under her bed. She bent to pick them up and Gilberto knelt beside her.

"I am so sorry, Angela. But you did not see what you think you saw." He reached for one of the chocolates but Angela pushed his hand away.

"I know what I saw, Gilberto. You and Gelah were holding holds."

Gilberto took Angela by the shoulders and gazed into her eyes. "I am Italian, Angela. Holding hands is part of my culture."

"Don't give me that," she shrieked. "Something is going on and you know it."

Gilberto let his hands fall. "*Sì,*" he admitted. "Something is going on."

"What?" demanded Angela.

"I cannot tell you," mumbled Gilberto. "Not yet. You will have to trust me."

Doctor Jonas entered the room, saw Angela on the floor and rushed to her side. "What happened? Are you all right?"

"Yes, I'm fine," replied Angela. "I just dropped a box of candy."

"Well, leave it for now," laughed the doctor. "I'll send someone in to clean it up later." She extended her hand and helped Angela to her feet. "And who is this distinguished-looking gentleman?"

Angela lay back in the bed. She didn't feel sick but all the excitement was taking its toll on her. "I'm sorry, Dr. Jonas. This is my husband, Gilberto."

"Well, I am pleased to meet you Mr. Fontero." She shook hands with Gilberto. "I'm glad you're here. I have Angela's test results and I think it is best you hear them."

14
DECISIONS

Dr. Jonas scanned Angela's chart. "When you came in yesterday, we did a routine ultrasound to try and determine the reason you fainted. Your heart and arteries were fine but we discovered a suspicious mass in your left breast. The biopsy I performed this morning was to determine if that mass was a cyst or something else. If I had only withdrawn liquid, we could have safely said the mass was a cyst. However, part of what I extracted was solid."

Angela grasped Gilberto's hand and squeezed.

"Now, that in itself isn't anything to worry about but I would like to take the examination one step further with a surgical biopsy."

Angela reacted quickly. "No. No surgery."

"We need to find out if the mass is cancerous and the only way to do that is with a more comprehensive test."

Sensing the doctor wasn't going to take

No for an answer, Angela took a deep breath. "What would you have to do?"

"There are two options. The quickest is to do a frozen section or cryosection. I would extract a small amount of tissue that would be rapidly frozen, sliced and examined while you were still in the operating room. The results would tell us if the mass is benign or malignant, but nothing else. The more accurate method is to perform a lumpectomy to remove the mass and part of the tissue around it. That way, a larger sample could be sent to the lab for a more thorough analysis. It takes 48 to 72 hours to get the results but we would have a better picture about what's going on."

"What if the mass is malignant?" Angela squeezed Gilberto's hand tighter.

"*If* it is, we would follow up with 5 or 6 weeks of radiation in order to eliminate any cancer cells that might still be present. The combination of a lumpectomy and radiation is commonly called breast-conserving therapy. It's less invasive than a mastectomy and the results are excellent."

"What if I decide against surgery?"

"There are alternative therapies you could try but you would be taking a chance by delaying. If the mass is malignant, the cancer could spread into other parts of your

195

body and once that happens, we would have to pursue more aggressive treatments."

"Do I need to decide right now?"

"Of course not. This is an important decision. Why don't you and your husband take some time to discuss it? I have surgery this morning but I can drop by after lunch. If you decide on the biopsy, I can do it tomorrow. If you decide against it, you'll be free to go home."

The doctor reached into her pocket and pulled out several pamphlets. "These might answer whatever questions you haven't already asked." She said her goodbyes and walked out of Angela's room.

Angela and Gilberto stared into each other's eyes. The rest of the world faded to black. It was just the two of them. Gilberto was the first to speak.

"You could die." His words were little more than a whisper.

Angela released Gilberto's hand, leaned back against the up-righted bed and closed her eyes. "Would you care?"

Gilberto turned his back and walked to the window. "When we married, it was for better or worse. Losing you would be the worst thing that could happen."

"No, it isn't, Gil. Losing you to another woman would be the worst."

Gilberto spun around and faced Angela. "There is no one else in my life, Angela. I love only you."

Her mind's eye played back the whole diner scene and rage took over. "Then what is going on between you and Gelah?"

"Nothing."

"Don't lie to me, Gil. I saw you with her."

Gilberto hung his head. "She is helping with a problem."

"What sort of problem?"

"I cannot tell you," he mumbled.

"Then why don't you just get out of here and leave me alone? I can make this decision without you."

Gilberto tried to embrace Angela but she pushed him away. She didn't want him anywhere around and she let it be known. "Just go."

He didn't look back as he left the room.

To her own amazement, Angela didn't cry. She'd been on her own before and she could do it again. She could stay on the farm and devote herself to taking care of the goats or she could move somewhere else and start over again. Either way, she would survive.

She picked up the pamphlets and began reading. One described the difference between a lumpectomy and mastectomy; another, what to expect after radiation and chemotherapy. Now there was a question she hadn't asked . . . was she going to need chemo? The one leaflet that captured her attention explained the emotional aspects of breast cancer. It said it was important to keep a positive attitude, accept that there were events she couldn't control and learn to relax.

"Oh sure, my entire world is blown to smithereens and you're telling me to relax. What's next? Take up yoga and knitting?" Just as she was about to throw the pamphlets across the room, the telephone rang.

"Hey, girlfriend, what are you doing in the hospital?" It was Katherine. "Need a timeout from that good-looking husband of yours?"

Angela finally broke into tears. "Oh, Katherine. My life is falling apart. I don't know which way to turn."

For the next hour, Angela poured her heart and soul out to her friend. She told her about Gil and Gelah, about the alligator dream and about the surgery. "You know how I am about doctors and hospitals. I stay as far away as possible. How can I let them cut me up just to find out whether or not I have cancer?"

"Because it could save your life." Katherine was adamant. "You can't let some nasty little cells take over your body. You've got to get them before they can get you."

"So you think I should have the surgery?"

"Absolutely. And everything else that goes along with it. Including the drugs."

"But what about Gil? Do you think he's cheating on me?"

"I don't know. I'll make that decision once I get there."

"You're coming up?" Angela was so excited she nearly cheered.

"Of course I am. After all, you invited me up for that Fall Festival, didn't you?"

"That's right. So much has happened that I'd forgotten about it."

"Well, I didn't. In fact, I've been practicing my hillbilly accent ever since you asked me. Mongo says he can't understand a word when I talk like that but I can't understand him when he speaks Cuban so I guess we're even."

Angela laughed. "You know something, Katherine. I really miss you."

"Me you, too. But we can spend every minute together once I get there."

"Well, let's not go overboard."

"Oh, hush," laughed Katherine. "Now you go ahead and let them do that lumpy thing and I'll call you tomorrow after it's all over.

And don't worry about Gil. I'll take care of him."

Talking with Katherine had raised Angela's spirits and changed her outlook. Before the call, she had been confused and depressed. Now she felt determined and confident. She knew what she had to do and she wasn't frightened about doing it. Maybe that pamphlet was right. Maybe Katherine was, too.

An old Fred Astaire-Ginger Rogers movie was playing when Dr. Jonas entered Angela's room later that afternoon. "Ahh, Fred and Ginger. Now, if we only had popcorn."

Angela smiled bravely. "I've decided to go with the biopsy."

"I hoped you would," replied the doctor. "I booked the operating room for eight tomorrow morning. That way you'll be finished and back in your room in time for lunch."

"Will I have to stay another night?" Angela wasn't looking forward to spending another night in the hospital. But then, what did she have to go home for?

"Let's just see how things go tomorrow and go from there."

During the night, someone removed Angela's water pitcher. Just before dawn, a nurse gave her a shot but no breakfast.

Around seven a.m., she was transferred to a gurney and wheeled down the hall to the elevator. She thought she felt Gilberto holding her hand but she wasn't sure. Nothing seemed normal. Her head was spinning and everything seemed to be moving in slow motion. In the operating room, a soft-spoken man asked her to count backwards from one hundred. She got to ninety-eight before Fred started dancing across the ceiling.

Someone patted her cheek. "Mrs. Fontero? Are you awake?"

Angela wondered why people were always trying to wake her up. Couldn't they let her finish her dreams? "Yeth." Her mouth felt like it was stuffed with cotton.

"Suck on this ice," said the voice. "We'll be taking you back to your room in a minute." The voice had a gentle face and it was smiling.

"What about the surgery?" asked Angela.

"You're all finished and your husband is in the waiting room. Would you like me to go get him?"

Even though she was still groggy, Angela had no trouble responding. "Not just yet, thank you. Give me time for my head to clear." *Like maybe a year or two.*

As soon as she was back in her room,

Angela spotted the difference. There was a large bouquet of yellow roses on the night-stand, three vases of mixed flowers on the tray table, two green plants on the sink counter and four Get-Well-Soon Mylar balloons floating across the ceiling toward the door. The flowers Gilberto brought the night before were on the windowsill and looked to be wilting in the sun. "Where'd all this come from?" she asked.

The teenager who wheeled her into the room shrugged. "Friends, prob'bly." His hair was spiked and sprayed hot pink. "Want I should read ya the cards?"

Angela mused over the boy's reading abilities and respectfully declined his offer. "It will give me something to do later."

After the pink-haired boy helped Angela into the bed, he rolled the gurney out of the room and left her alone. Her throat hurt, probably from the anesthesia, but her head was clearing. She raised her hand to her breast and felt the bandage. It covered most of her chest but there was no pain. Would that come later? She leaned back against the pillows and looked up at the ceiling. The balloons had moved away from the door and were now hovering over her bed. Were they following her?

Bobby Jo, the candy striper, poked her

head in the doorway. "Back already?"

"Yes," replied Angela. "I just got back a few minutes ago."

"Like the way I set up your flowers?"

"You did this?" Angela surveyed the room.

"Yeah. I thought it would make you feel good when you got back."

"Well, it did. Thank you so much." Angela rubbed her wrist. "What time is it, anyway? They wouldn't let me wear my watch."

"Going on eleven," announced the girl. "They should be bringing your lunch soon."

"Great. I'm starving."

As if on cue, an orderly carried in a tray and pushed the vases aside in order to place it on Angela's tray table. In the process, one vase tipped over but Bobby Jo grabbed it before it hit the ground.

"Good catch," cheered Angela.

"Thanks," replied Bobby Jo. "I play volleyball in the summer so I'm used to moving fast."

"Really?" Angela enjoyed the girl's company. She was chatty without being nosey, bright without being brainy, and cute without being glamorous. Would her daughter have been like that? She studied her lunch. There was a turkey and Swiss sandwich with a side of pasta salad, a cup of what looked to be vegetable soup, a small bowl of green grapes, apple slices and fresh straw-berries, a pot of hot tea and a chocolate brownie.

"I had to order for you again," apologized the girl. "Hope you don't mind."

"Everything looks delicious, Bobby Jo. Maybe I'll make you my personal chef." Angela regretted her words the moment they were spoken. She already had a chef and look how that turned out. She pushed the rolling table away and turned away to hide her eyes.

"Are you okay, Mrs. Fontero?" The candy striper looked alarmed.

"Yes, I'm fine," lied Angela. "It's just that my throat is kind of sore. Maybe lunch wasn't such a good idea, after all."

"How about the soup?" asked the girl. "That might make it feel better."

"Maybe later." Angela tried to clear her throat. It felt like someone had used a nail file on it. She didn't want lunch and she didn't want to chat. All she wanted was to be left alone. "Right now, I think I'd like to take a nap."

"Oh. Sure." Bobby Jo backed away from Angela's bed. "Maybe I'll stop back later."

Angela nodded but didn't say anything. What was wrong with her? She chased Monica off yesterday, Gilberto when he'd shown up, and now this innocent girl who was only trying to be friendly. Was that what she'd been doing her whole life? Running away from people and situations she couldn't face?

The pattern was all too familiar. Finally out of her teens, she'd exercised her hard-gained independence and gotten pregnant hoping the baby's father, a married man with two children, would whisk her away from her loveless family. When that didn't happen, she gave the child up rather than face her parents' wrath. Ten years later, she married her first husband thinking he would exorcise her demons. All he did was bring more pain into her life. That was when she gave up on men and started rescuing dogs. Dogs were loyal, they didn't talk back and they never told lies. But even dogs had a downside — landlords didn't want them on their property. That was why she ended up in Florida.

Angela flicked on the TV hoping to find something to drown out her nagging thoughts. An afternoon talk show host was interviewing a glamorous blonde starlet who was wearing a sequined dress. She didn't hear a word they said.

Florida was supposed to have been a temporary solution until she could figure out what to do with her remaining years. She was already in her sixties. She hadn't intended on meeting anyone, or getting involved. And getting married? That had been the last thing on her mind. She hadn't wanted to take a chance on another man but, somehow, it happened and now she had to deal with the consequences. The question was how.

Angela was reaching for the telephone when Dr. Jonas walked into her room.

"How are you feeling, Angela?" The doctor wore her usual smile and white smock.

"Not bad," replied Angela. "My throat is sore but that's about all."

"Well, good. The surgery went well and I was able to remove the entire cyst."

"Does that mean I can go home?"

"Not yet. Your blood pressure was a little high during the procedure so I would like to keep you one more night for observation."

Angela frowned. "Is something wrong with my heart?"

"No," replied the doctor. "We ruled that out with the ultrasound. It's just that the anticipation of surgery causes some patients stress and stress can increase blood pressure. As your body gets back to normal, you might experience a little pain and that could raise your blood pressure again. We're better equipped to deal with that here in the hospital than you would be if you were back in the hollows."

Knowing the doctor was probably right, Angela gave in. "Okay, but just one more night, right?"

"Yes," agreed the doctor, "just one. In fact, go ahead and tell your family to pick you up tomorrow morning around ten. That way you can have a leisurely breakfast and I can have one final look before you're on your way. How does that sound?"

"Great," replied Angela.

Once the doctor left, Angela reached for the telephone again and dialed her home number. After letting it ring ten times, she disconnected and dialed Steve and Monica's number. No one answered there either. Where was everyone? She considered calling Gelah but decided against it. I'll cross that bridge when I get there. Just as she was about to call Pam, Monica walked in.

"How'd it go?" asked Monica.

"Okay," replied Angela. "Dr. Jonas said she removed the cyst and that I can go home tomorrow morning. Only thing is I can't get a hold of Gil. Have you seen him?"

A puzzled look crossed Monica's face. "Don't you know?"

"Know what?" asked Angela.

"He drove down to Alabama last night."

"Alabama?" Angela felt her face flush. Maybe it was a good thing she was still in the hospital. With everything Gilberto was putting her through she might need emergency care. "What on earth for?"

"I don't know. He just said he had important business to take care of."

"Did he go alone?"

Monica hesitated then slowly shook her head. "Gelah went with him."

Angela's worst fear had come true. Gil was cheating on her. Fighting the impulse to crawl into the nearest hole, she made up her mind. This time, she wasn't going to run.

15
COMING HOME

The house was eerily quiet when Angela entered. The windows were shut, the shades were drawn and there was no one around to welcome her. On the way back from the hospital, Monica explained she was keeping Gizmo down at the main house because, "ever since the goats escaped he seems to have grown very protective of them."

Even though Angela was grateful Monica was taking good care of her dog, not having him or Gilberto around was disturbing, almost frightening. She walked through the rooms looking for something, anything, to distract or comfort her. But there was only silence. She caught a glimpse of herself in the hall mirror. Her ponytail looked longer and grayer. Could being in the hospital a couple of days do that? Turning to the side, she studied her chest. The bandages hid the surgery. *Will I be lopsided once they're removed?* Needing the reassurance of another living being, she fled the house in search of her only solace — her dog.

As she neared their house, Angela noticed Steve and Monica standing by the goat pen. Monica was pointing. "Couldn't we extend the fence up the hill?"

Steve shook his head. "No. They'd probably just crawl under it like they did down here."

"Who crawled under what?" asked Angela.

"Dogs." Monica planted her hands on her hips and scanned the hill beyond the pen. "Steve says a pack of wild dogs attacked the goats while we were in town."

Angela's hand shot to her mouth. "Oh, no. Were any of them hurt?"

Steve nodded. "One of the dogs nipped Sophia but Gizmo ran him and his buddies off before they could do any more real harm."

"Where's Gizmo now?" Angela looked around the pen. Her dog was nowhere in sight — nor were any of the goats.

"I moved him and the goats into the milking shed so I could check and see where the dogs went." He raised the rifle leaning against a fence post.

"What's that for?" Angela didn't like guns and nearly went ballistic when Gilberto mentioned he was going to buy one so he could go hunting with Steve.

"Just in case." Steve's expression was somber.

"Good thinking, preacher man." Monica patted her husband's back then grabbed Angela's arm and tugged. "Let's go let those goats out before they wreck the place."

The two women raced toward the shed. Angela arrived first and jerked the door open. Inside, Bucky and two females stood quietly in one corner while Gizmo and Sophia lay alongside the milking stanchion. Gizmo was licking Sophia's leg.

"Will you look at that?" Angela stepped aside so Monica could see what was happening.

"See," chuckled Monica. "I told you he was being protective."

Angela got on her knees and hugged her dog while Monica inspected the goat's injured leg.

"The skin is barely broken," declared Monica. "Hand me the Bag Balm. That should make our little girl feel better."

Angela buried her head in the scruff of Gizmo's neck and started crying.

"What's wrong?" asked Monica.

"Nothing. Everything. I just don't know anymore." Angela's sobs were punctuated with hiccups.

Monica sat next to Angela. "You've been through a lot, Angela. The move, the goats, your surgery. No one expects you to know what to do."

Angela wiped her nose on her elbow. "You didn't mention Gil."

Monica interlaced her fingers with Angela's. "There's an old prayer about living one day at a time and having the wisdom to know the difference between the things you can and cannot change. Whatever decisions Gil makes in his life are entirely his own and you can't change them. The decision you have to make right now is to get well. Can you do that? For me?"

Angela studied Monica's face. There was a time when she didn't like this woman, when she thought she was stern and uncompromising. She considered Monica to be the type of person you respected or feared, sort of like the nuns back in grade school. But there she was, sitting smack-dab in the middle of a nannyberry-covered floor, begging her to get well. "For you?"

"Yes," whispered Monica. "Me. Don't you know how important you are to me?"

Angela shook her head. At the moment, she didn't feel important to anyone.

"When we first met, I thought you were just another divorcee after my husband."

"Me? After Steve?" Had her infatuation been that transparent?

"Yes. But when I got to know you, I realized you were going through some pretty rough times and needed a friend. Sure, you had Tony and Fran but Tony acted more like a father than a brother."

Angela smiled and nodded in agreement. She wondered what had kept her and Tony apart as kids. There wasn't that much difference in their ages — twenty-two months to be exact. Yet Tony never acted like a kid. It was like there was always something else going on in his life. Sure, he taught her how to ride a bike and even took her camping a couple of times but he never really played with her. Why?

Monica laughed. "Remember the time we went to that basketball game and you got all flustered when everyone started kidding you about becoming one of those senior cheerleaders?"

Angela remembered the night. It was the first time she'd been out with Gilberto and she was nervous. "I think it was Gil that brought that up."

"The expression on your face was priceless. You looked half intrigued and half scared to death."

"Well, the whole thing was ridiculous."

Angela loosened her fingers and started petting Gizmo. Probably relieved that his guard duties were fulfilled, he rolled over on his side.

Monica sighed and gazed at the shed ceiling. "I think that's when I started thinking of you as a sister."

Angela's eyes blossomed into saucers. "A sister?"

"Yeah. I never had one when I was growing up and when I entered the convent everyone was so busy trying to be devout we never got to know one another." Running her fingers through her hair, Monica unearthed a blade of straw. Checking to see if there were more, she continued talking. "Steve and I started out like brother and sister in Nicaragua but that quickly changed."

Angela grinned. "You know, I've always wondered about that."

"Long story," chuckled Monica. "Maybe some other time. Right now, I just want you to know that no matter what happens, I'm here for you."

No one had ever told her that before. Not when she was going through her pregnancy, not when she was going through her divorce, and certainly not when she was packing up to move out of Indiana. She'd weathered all of her storms alone and survived, but now that she knew someone was standing by to help her, she felt relieved. A quiet knock distracted her from hugging Monica.

"Sorry to interrupt," said Steve. "But Angela has visitors."

All of the bible school students stood patiently waiting outside the shed door. They looked so nice. The Walton boys were wearing clean jeans and had their hair slicked back. Several girls were wearing cotton dresses. Florence was carrying a large silver container.

"Ya missed out on the ice cream," said Florence, "so my Mamaw made this fer you." The little girl offered the container to Angela and peaked over her eyebrows to see if she would accept it. "It be black walnut," she said. "Ya likes black walnut, doncha?"

Angela took the container. It was still cold enough that her fingertips stuck to it. "I've never had it," she confessed, "but I'm willing to try." A vision of Gilberto sharing his gelato flashed through her mind. How long ago had that been?

"Let's take it up to the house," suggested Monica. "I'll get some bowls and spoons and we can all give it a try."

Back at the house, no one waited for bowls — everyone just dug their spoons into the frosty container and began devouring its contents. Little Florence bragged that her Mamaw used the last of her black walnuts to make the ice cream.

Thinking how much of a hardship that might have been, Angela said she would buy more the next time she went into town.

The children exploded into laughter.

Aware she must have made some sort of mistake, Angela smiled. It felt good to know the children felt comfortable enough to laugh. It was a sign they had accepted her . . . maybe not as an equal but at least as a friend.

"Ya don't buy black walnuts," giggled Florence, "ya go out an pick 'em . . . fer free."

Struggling to keep a straight face, one of Pam's boys explained how it was done. "Ya back a pickup truck up to a tree, whack the tree trunk a couple times with the back bumper and then stand back when the walnuts start fallin'. Ya would'n wanna get hit in the haid by one'a them babies."

"Really?" Angela knew the boy was as good a storyteller as his father and she wanted to hear more.

"Sure," replied the boy. "That's the whole idea behind the Harvest Festival. Did'n you know that?"

"I knew about the festival," admitted Angela, "but I thought it was all about farm harvests, not walnuts."

"There was a story about it in yesterday's paper," added Steve. "I guess walnut harvesting is a major source of income in this county."

"Yeah," said one of the other boys. "Between walnuts and 'coons, my pappy and I made nuff money las cheer to buy us a used tractor. The guy we bought it off even traded us a grader blade fer a load'a walnuts."

"That's amazing," said Steve. "Do you have to have a permit to collect the nuts?"

"Nope," replied the boy. "Jist a truck."

Anyone watching would have seen the wheels turning in Steve's head. "Hmm. I wonder how many truckloads it would take to buy a new woodstove for the church."

One of the girls said her father worked at the co-op. "Maybe he could get us a deal."

Angela realized the girl said *us*. She, like the other children, had worked all summer in order to make Camp Gizmo a success. They had taken good care of Gizmo and the goats, they grew enough vegetables to feed several hungry families and they even made enough money to buy a new church bell. Now, when the only thing they should

217

be thinking about was school, they were looking for ways to keep their little group together. *Why?* Aside from the satisfaction of doing something worthwhile, how did they benefit? Free food and ice cream? No. It was something else. It was friendship and the feeling of belonging. Two things that everyone needed . . . including her.

After finishing the last of the ice cream, Sharon's girls offered to walk little Florence home and Pam's boys volunteered to keep them company. When all the children were gone, Angela leaned her head back and sighed.

"You look tired," said Monica.

"A little," confessed Angela.

"Would you like to take a nap? The living room couch is really comfortable and I could drag out a quilt."

"Sounds good but I think I'll just get Gizmo and head home." Her stitches were beginning to hurt and she was wearing the same clothes she'd worn the day they took her to the hospital — the day she'd seen Gilberto and Gelah together at the diner. More than a nap, she needed to wash away every memory of that day. She needed to feel clean.

"Need a lift?" asked Steve.

"Thanks but after three days in the hospital, the fresh air will do me good."

Angela hugged Steve and Monica, called for Gizmo and began the short hike up the hill to her house. As she reached the top of the ridge, she heard the telephone. It was her ring. Leaving Gizmo to fend for himself, she sprinted the rest of the way, tore through the house and grabbed the phone. "Hello?" No response. "Hello?" Nothing but a dial tone. Whoever was calling had hung up. "Just my luck," she muttered.

Gizmo found his way into the kitchen and nudged his empty water bowl.

Angela patted his head and apologized. "Sorry, boy. It must have dried up while you were down at Monica's. Wonder what else happened while I was gone?"

She filled the dog's bowl, gave him a couple doggy treats and was raising the window shades when the phone rang again. This time she answered on the second ring.

"Where have you been?" demanded the caller. "I've been calling all morning."

"Katherine? Is that you?" It sounded like Katherine but something was different. Was she in a tunnel?

"Of course, it's me. Whom were you expecting? Publisher's Clearing House?"

"Well, no . . ."

"I called the hospital but they said you

219

were already discharged. What did they find out? How are you feeling?"

"They probably won't have the test results until the middle of next week but I'm feeling fine. Just a little sore."

"Well, don't worry about a thing. Mongo and I are on the way."

"What do you mean *on the way?*"

"We're in the . . . on the . . . you know . . . the road."

"What's wrong with your phone, Katherine? I'm only getting every other word."

"It's a . . . cell. Wait, we'll pull . . ."

The phone went dead. Angela looked at it for a few seconds then placed the receiver in its cradle. When she started to walk away, it rang again

"Katherine?"

"Yes, it's me. I hate cell phones but Mongo insisted we weren't going anywhere without one. 'What if we break down?' he said. 'What if we get stranded on the top of a snowy mountain somewhere?' That man worries about the craziest things. Imagine — snow in September? Sometimes I wonder why I even married him."

"You're babbling, Katherine. Slow down and tell me where you are."

"Just north of Jacksonville. If we make it to Savannah tonight, we'll be there by tomorrow afternoon."

"Where? Here?"

"Of course there. You invited me, didn't you?"

"Yes, but I thought you weren't coming until next weekend."

"That was the original plan but I decided to leave early so we could have more time together. You don't mind, do you?"

"No, that's great. It's just that I haven't gotten the trailer ready and I'm moving kind of slow right now."

"Don't worry about the trailer. I can take care of it when I get there. Or, better yet, get Gil to do it."

Angela wasn't ready to tell Katherine all the latest details so she just laughed. "Yeah, like that's going to happen."

"Well, whatever. Just don't sweat it, okay? The only thing I want you to worry about for the next couple of days is getting well."

Katherine was the second person to say that today. Just when she felt like she'd lost her last friend, she discovered there were still plenty of them around. And they were all concerned about her. Even the children.

Some great writer once said that a friend was a person who listened to all your problems then blew them away with one breath of kindness. That's what her friends were doing — blowing her cares away with kindness. Where was Gil? What was he doing? Why was he with Gelah?

16
KATHERINE

Katherine's arrival in the hollow turned into a major event. The convertible top of her tricked-out, red Beetle was rolled down, the radio was blaring full blast, and Katherine was standing up singing John Denver's *Country Roads* and throwing candy to all the curious children who ran to the road to see what the commotion was about. Mongo had his baseball cap pulled so far down over his face it was a miracle he could see to drive the car.

Angela heard her friends coming even before they reached the mailboxes. That was more than a mile away. She grinned, grabbed a sweater and ran down to the road. Waving her arms over her head, she flagged them down just as they were turning the bend.

Mongo slammed on the brakes but Katherine jumped out before he could bring the little car to a stop. The children chasing behind shouted and attempted to catch her but, like a cat, she landed on her feet and sprinted toward Angela.

"Angela, Angela." Screaming like a banshee, the redhead wrapped Angela in a bear hug.

"Ouch." Angela pulled away and touched her breast. "Stitches. Remember?"

Katherine frowned and narrowed her eyes. "Stitches? We don' need no stinkin' stitches." She hugged Angela again, this time more gently, and Angela hugged back. Mongo stayed in the car and shook his head like a disapproving traffic cop.

"Come on," said Angela, "Let's drop your things at the trailer and go for a walk. I want to show you around."

"Great. I came prepared." Katherine pointed at her red gym shoes.

"Where did you find those?"

"The Carol Wright catalog. Like 'em?"

"Oh, yeah," mocked Angela. "I wish I had a pair."

"I was hoping you'd say that." Katherine turned toward the car, opened the truck and pulled out a shoebox. "You're a size eight, right?"

Wondering what the neighbors would think if they saw her in red shoes, Angela opened the box and gasped. "Yellow? You got me yellow sneakers?"

"They didn't have your size in red," said Katherine. "But I figured you probably wore a lot of denim and yellow goes good with denim. Right?"

Angela couldn't argue with that logic. It made a lot of sense . . . even for Katherine. "I love them." She stuck the box under her arm and waved for Mongo to follow.

When they reached the trailer, Katherine hesitated. "Kinda small, isn't it?"

"Well, it's not the Ritz but it's comfortable."

Responding to Angela's not-so-gentle poke in the ribs, Katherine stepped inside the trailer, looked left and right and asked, "Where's the bathroom?"

Stifling a smirk, Angela innocently answered, "Out back. That won't be a problem. Will it?"

Katherine's face went blank. Taking a deep breath, she glared at Angela. "I'll get you for this, Mrs. Fontero. I don't know how yet but rest assured, I will get you."

Angela glared back. "Yeah? You and who else?"

"How 'bout me?" shouted Monica.

Katherine jumped from the trailer and ran toward Monica. "Save me. Save me. This crazy woman wants to lock me up in that sardine can and it doesn't even have a bath-room."

Monica draped her arm across Angela's shoulders and taunted Katherine. "Did she also tell you you'd have to bathe in the river?"

Katherine's mouth dropped. "The river?"

Angela was pleased Monica had shown up. She'd been doing a lot of that lately . . . showing up where she was least expected. But that's what family did, wasn't it? They just showed up when they sensed another family member needed help. And she said she thought of Angela as a sister. Maybe she could shield her from Katherine's inevitable questions about Gilberto.

Monica laughed. "You're not afraid of snakes, are you?"

"That does it." Katherine stomped back to her car. "Mongo? Turn this thing around. We're going home."

Mongo nodded but didn't react. Angela and Monica grabbed Katherine's arms and wrestled her to the ground.

"You'll stay right here," commanded Monica. "If it's good enough for us, it's good enough for you."

Katherine pretended to struggle but suddenly started laughing. Angela and Monica let loose of her arms and helped her up.

Mongo slid the baseball cap farther down his face and quietly mumbled *women.*

"Listen," said Monica, "if you really don't like the trailer, you can stay in my upstairs bedroom. The bathroom is on the first floor but there's a great view of the goat yard out the windows."

Katherine wrinkled her nose. "Charming. Which way does the wind blow?"

"Away from the house," replied Monica. ". . . Usually."

"Oh, gee," scoffed Katherine. "Which sounds more inviting? Bathing with snakes or smelling goats all night? It's *so* hard to choose."

Monica pointed toward her house. "I've got a bottle of wine in the cooler maybe that will help you decide."

Katherine leaned sideways and whispered in Angela's ear. "Did she say cooler?"

Walking toward the bridge, Angela motioned for her friend to follow. "You'll see."

"What about Mongo?" asked Katherine.

Angela turned around and started walking backwards. "He can come, too but tell him to leave the car where it is. We try not to drive heavy things over the bridge too often. You never know when it might give away."

"Good grief, Angela. What have you gotten me into?"

"Come on."

Angela ran across the bridge. Katherine and Mongo followed, much more slowly. When they were all gathered around Monica's kitchen table, she opened the wine and apologized that Steve wasn't at home. "He went into town to talk to a man at the co-op."

Katherine sipped her wine. "Oh yeah?" She turned to Angela. "Did Gil go with?"

Angela played with some imaginary crumbs on the table. "No. He's in Alabama."

Katherine emptied her glass and pushed it toward Monica for a refill. "Alabama?"

"Yes. He said he had business there."

"What kind of business?" asked Katherine.

"I don't know," barked Angela. "Can't we talk about something else?"

"See," Katherine poked Mongo's arm causing him to spill his wine. "I told you something was wrong."

Monica grabbed a towel from the back of her chair and mopped up the spilt wine. Coming to Angela's defense, she insisted that nothing was wrong. "He said he had something important to take care of and that he'd be back in a couple of days."

Katherine directed her attention to Angela. "What did he tell you?"

"I didn't talk to him." Angela's temper was reaching the boiling point. She raised her wineglass to her mouth but put it back on the table without drinking. "He didn't even tell me he was going."

All eyes were on Angela. *These are my friends,* she thought. *I can't dump on them like this. It isn't fair.* Raising her chin, she turned toward Katherine. "So, what's it gonna be? The tin can or the goat yard?"

Looking like a deer caught in headlights, Katherine stammered. "Ah, I haven't seen the bedroom yet. Maybe I should go look?"

"Oh, sure." Monica rose from her chair. "Right this way, my lady."

When Katherine and Monica were gone, Mongo placed his hand on top of Angela's. "Would you like to talk?" he asked.

Angela realized it was the first time Mongo had spoken directly to her or shown any signs of friendship. He had always been the crazy Cuban who drank too much and carried his wife's purse around. Did he have another side or was he just trying to make small talk?

"Oh, you don't want to listen to my problems," said Angela.

Mongo cupped both hands around his half-empty wineglass. "Yes. I do. You are my wife's friend and what affects you, affects her. Tell me, what has Gilberto done that upsets you so?" The wine bottle was sitting in the middle of the table but he made no attempt to refill his glass.

Angela told Mongo the whole story — all her uncertainties, all her suspicions, all her worries. She told him why she was worried — how her first husband cheated on her and how the second was following suit. She told him she felt like she was caught up in some sort of weird déjà vu whirlwind and didn't know how to get out. She even told him about her dreams and how real they seemed. It felt liberating to get everything off her chest, especially to someone who was almost a stranger. Sure, he was Katherine's husband but they were never really friends. Until now.

When Angela was finished unburdening her deepest secrets, she noticed tears streaking down Mongo's face. She had never seen him cry. She had never seen Gilberto cry, either. *Could he?*

Katherine tromped down the stairs and declared she and Mongo would be staying in Monica's spare bedroom. "You should see the place. It's huge. And the windows don't just overlook the goat yard, they overlook the whole countryside." Noticing

Mongo's tears and Angela's sad expression, she asked if she had interrupted anything.

"No," lied Mongo. "We were just talking about old times and how much we missed each other."

Katherine shook her head. "Super. My best friend and husband crying together over a bottle of wine. That's what I love about you guys. You're both softies." She kissed the top of Angela's head and nudged Mongo's shoulder. "Go get the bags and take them up to our room. Monica says dinner won't be ready for another two hours. That'll give Angela enough time to take me on that tour she promised."

"Wouldn't you rather rest up?" Angela felt drained after her talk with Mongo. Going for a walk was the last thing on her mind.

"Nope. I rested all the way up. Now I want to see what it is you love about this place."

"Go ahead," said Monica. "I'll help Mongo get the bags then he can help me with dinner. Deal?"

"Deal," agreed Mongo.

Instead of following the road, Angela took a short cut to the ridge — straight up the hill. Within minutes, Katherine was huffing and puffing. "You seem to have forgotten the only exercise I get is chasing waiters."

"That's why I decided to take this way. You looked like you needed a good workout."

Katherine plopped down next to a tree. "What are you, my personal trainer?"

Angela grabbed Katherine's hand and pulled her to her feet. "Come on, the house is just ahead. And brush those ants off your pants. They might bite."

Swatting her rear end, Katherine stumbled up the hill. "They're not red ants, are they?"

"No," laughed Angela. "But they bite just as hard." She raced after Katherine.

In less than a week, Angela's entire life had changed. She found out she might have cancer, she lost a piece of her body, and she didn't know where her husband was. While she was in the hospital, Monica had taken over milking duties and made sure Gizmo was walked at least once a day. Being able to get outside and walk the hills renewed her strength. It was the first time in days she felt she could breathe. She felt rejuvenated.

When they reached the top of the ridge, Angela pointed out her flowerbeds, the cemetery and the view. "Steve and Monica's church is down there and my friend Pam's place is over there. Sharon Schuster and her family live down the hollow from

Pam but you can't see their place from here."

"Are you happy here?" asked Katherine.

Angela sighed. "I thought I was, but that was before all this cancer business."

"You're going to be fine, Angela. Mark my word."

"I hope you're right." Angela more than hoped, she prayed.

"So, what's going on between you and Gil?" Katherine had a habit of going straight to the heart of a matter.

"The usual. He's found someone else." Angela tried to act matter-of-fact but the quiver in her voice gave her away.

"Are you sure?" asked Katherine.

"I saw them together."

"Where?"

"In town." Angela wondered why Katherine wasn't being more supportive. She should have been consoling her instead of asking a bunch of questions. "Listen, Katherine. I'm really not in the mood to talk about this. Let's talk about you. What's happening in your life?"

"Mongo and I are selling our trailer and Tony got arrested for his fourth DUI."

"Whoa. One thing at a time. *What* happened to Tony?" Last year, he had been rushed to the hospital after passing out at

Thanksgiving dinner. The doctors told him he had high blood sugar and should quit drinking. Having been arrested for his fourth DUI meant he had ignored their orders.

"The cops stopped him outside of Fort Lauderdale. Evidently he and Fran had a terrible fight and he went to a bar to drown his sorrows."

"He and Fran were arguing?" Angela couldn't remember ever hearing Fran so much as raise her voice. What could have driven her to argue?

"Yeah. They've been doing a lot of that lately. Everyone in the park is talking about it. She wants him to go to rehab but he says he doesn't have a drinking problem."

Angela nodded. "He tells me the same thing."

"Anyway, he went to one of those bars down on the beach, had five or six drinks and got so obnoxious the bartender called the cops. By the time they arrived he had left the bar, started driving home and ended up ramming his truck into a palm tree."

"Was he hurt?"

"A few scratches but nothing serious. He spent the night in jail because Fran refused to bail him out. Said maybe it would teach him a lesson."

Angela looked off to the west. The sun was beginning to set and the golden leaves of the hickories seemed to glimmer in the fading light. The year was slipping away. She couldn't wait for it to be over. "When did all this happen?"

"A couple of weeks ago."

"Why didn't you tell me?"

Katherine shrugged her shoulders and walked toward the house. "I had other things to worry about."

"Like what?" Angela hurried to catch up.

"Well, *you* for one thing. Moving for another."

They reached the porch and sat on the steps. Angela brushed some leaves away and noticed a cocoon attached to one. Gently picking it up, she examined the papery casing. *What's inside?* she wondered. *A butterfly? A bagworm? I should save it and ask Gelah.* Remembering the diner, she let the leaf fall from her hand.

"Where are you moving to?"

"Cuba."

Confusion filled Angela's eyes. "Cuba? Why Cuba?"

"Mongo misses his family and since our best friends moved to West Virginia, there's no reason to stay in Florida."

"I'll never see you again."

"They have airplanes, Angela."

"I know but it's so far." Angela felt like she was losing everything. Her husband ran off with a woman who was supposed to be a friend, the Camp Gizmo children were going back to school, and the woman she depended upon, the woman she most wanted to be like, just told her she was moving to a foreign country. Not even a country . . . an island. A communist island. Who would she have left? Monica? Steve? The neighbors?

Katherine grinned. "Let's not worry about Cuba right now. Let's just kick back and enjoy each other's company. Hey . . . here's an idea." She pointed her left index finger toward the sky. "How about after dinner, I come back up here and spend the night with you. We could have a slumber party and talk the night away. It would do as both some good."

"What about Mongo?"

"A night alone isn't going to kill him. Besides, he'll see enough of me in Cuba."

"Well . . . if you think it's all right . . ." At least she wouldn't be alone.

"Okay. It's settled. The only question is do we have enough popcorn and chocolate to last through the night?"

Angela raised her eyebrows. "I don't know.

Let's check it out."

The two friends dashed into the house.

17

THINGS THAT GO BUMP . . .

Much to Mongo's displeasure, Katherine packed an overnight back and headed down the stairs. "It's just one night," she muttered. "Can't you get along without me that long?"

Steve, Monica and Angela watched from the front door as Mongo hung his head and submissively followed his wife.

"Steve is gonna walk us home," whined Angela. "Guess he's afraid we'll get lost or something."

Monica shook her finger. "Better safe than sorry. You could run into a mountain lion . . . or worse."

"Eek," screamed Katherine. "Lions and tigers and bears . . ."

"Oh, my." Angela locked arms with Katherine and skipped ahead of Steve.

When they reached Angela's house, Katherine stood in the doorway, stretched her arms and spread her feet. "Girls only," she ordered. "No boys allowed."

Steve grinned. "Don't you want me to check inside to make sure no one's hiding in there?"

Angela moved into position next to Katherine and helped block the way. "Of course not. That's Gizmo's job."

"Yeah," agreed Katherine. "He might be half-blind but he doesn't miss a thing."

Admitting defeat, Steve backed back away from the women. "Okay, have it your way. Just remember, if you need me, I'm only a phone call away."

Katherine shot Steve a condescending grin and smug beauty queen wave. "Good night, Steve. Sorry to see you go."

When Steve was finally out of earshot, Katherine turned to Angela and whispered one word . . . *Chocolate*.

Struggling to see who could get through the door first, the women raced for the kitchen. Claiming victory, Katherine immediately began tearing through the cabinets.

"Where is it?" she screeched.

Angela pushed her friend aside and opened the microwave. "In here."

Katherine frowned in disbelief. "The microwave?"

"I didn't want the mice to get it," chuckled Angela

"You have mice? In the kitchen?" Katherine backed away from the microwave and nervously examined the countertop.

"Sure. Doesn't everyone?" Ignoring Katherine's worried look, Angela instructed her to take the graham crackers and marshmallows out of an overhead cabinet.

"What? You weren't worried about the mice getting them?"

"I thought *this* was more important." Like a servant bearing her master's precious jewels, Angela held out a two-pound slab of milk chocolate. "Think it will be enough?"

Katherine lowered her nose to the chocolate and inhaled. "I have died and gone to heaven."

After filling a plate with s'mores and zapping them in the microwave, Katherine and Angela grabbed some paper napkins, retreated to the living room, placed the plate in the middle of the coffee table and sat cross-legged on the floor.

Chocolate dribbled down Katherine's chin as she bit into one of the s'mores. "Well, I never thought I'd be sitting in the middle of your living room eating s'mores. This is so much fun."

Angela sighed and placed her snack on a

napkin. "Yeah, fun." If things had been different, she might have been sitting with Gil and he might have been feeding her the gooey mess. If things had been different, she might not have seen him and Gelah together. If things had been different, she might not be facing the ordeal of cancer. But things weren't different and she had to accept the fact her life had changed . . . perhaps irreparably.

As if sensing her friend's anguish, Katherine reached across the table. "You're not alone, Angela." Placing her chocolate-smeared fingers on top of Angela's, she gently squeezed.

Angela swallowed the knot growing in her throat. "What am I going to do, Katherine?" Tears ran from her eyes but she didn't sob.

"First things first," replied Katherine. "Start by telling me what happened and then we'll figure out what to do."

Two pounds of chocolate and an hour later, Angela was finished relating her tale of woe. Feeling relieved, she breathed a heavy sigh and tried to smile. "So, what should I do old wise one?"

Katherine's expression was pensive. "Gil loves you, Angela. He would never do anything to hurt you."

"But . . ."

"But, nothing," interrupted Katherine. "He once told me he thought he would never find love again then he met you and it was like someone had given him a whole new lease on life. Men like that don't cheat."

Angela's eyes were glued to the table.

"He said you were the best thing that ever happened to him and his only fear was he wouldn't be able to give back half the love you gave him."

"Gil said that?"

"Yes and . . ."

The unexpected sounds of barking dogs tore through the quiet night.

"What's that?" asked Katherine.

"Hunters." Angela pushed away from the coffee table and walked toward the window. Katherine jumped up and tiptoed behind.

"At night?"

"Yeah, it's a little early in the season but nighttime is when they go after raccoons."

"But it's dark out there. How can they see them?"

"They use flashlights," replied Angela. "Come on, let's go out on the porch and see if we can spot them."

"Shouldn't we take Gizmo?" Katherine hesitated and pointed at the dog sleeping by the front door.

Gizmo raised his head as if saying, "I ain't going."

Katherine cringed and followed Angela outside.

Staying within the light of the living room windows, Angela told Katherine to stay where the hunters could see her and to listen closely.

"For what?"

"You'll see."

A steady breeze ruffled the wind chimes and chilled the night air. Somewhere in the distance, a melancholy whistle blew as a train made its way through the ridges. Thick clouds hung low in the sky, concealing the evening stars and filling the hollow with an eerie mist. Suddenly, a soft chirping followed by the baying of two fast-moving dogs shattered the silence. Craning their necks, Angela and Katherine tried to pinpoint where the sounds were coming from. A darting flashlight beam indicated the river. The dogs stopped running but continued barking as a shaft of light danced through the top of a tree. A few seconds later, a gunshot blast. Then everything was quiet.

"What just happened?" whispered Katherine.

"The dogs treed a raccoon and the hunter shot it."

"So, that's it? He takes his dogs, goes home and there's no more shooting?"

Angela shook her head. "No. Steve says they're not supposed to take more than four raccoons but a lot of hunters keep going as long as their dogs don't give out."

A gentle rain started to fall. "Maybe that will stop them," Katherine held her hand out to catch a few drops.

"I doubt it," replied Angela. "But let's get inside before we get drenched."

"Great idea. Is there any chocolate left?"

"No," laughed Angela. "But I've got plenty of popcorn."

Katherine frowned. "Well, if that's all you've got, I guess it will have to do."

While Angela popped the corn, Katherine retrieved a can of root beer and a pint of ice cream from the refrigerator. Half-filling two glasses with soda, she added the ice cream and giggled as foam slithered across the countertop. Angela smirked but didn't scold her friend. It felt good to leave her worries behind . . . at least for the moment.

The rain was getting heavier and the wind was picking up. When everything was ready, the women returned to the coffee table.

"Almost feels like camping, doesn't it?" asked Angela.

"I wouldn't know," jeered Katherine.

"The closest I ever get to camping is a Holiday Inn."

The crack of thunder echoed through the hollow. Then the lights went dead. Gizmo deserted his spot by the door and crawled under the coffee table.

"This always happens when it rains," said Angela.

"Wonderful. Do you have a generator?"

"No, but I've got candles." Angela shuffled back to the darkened kitchen, rummaged through a drawer and extracted two candles and a box of matches. Quickly returning to the living room, she lit the candles and placed them in the candleholders she kept on the coffee table.

The clatter of rain beating against the tin roof made normal conversation almost impossible. "Good thing you're not down at the trailer," shouted Angela.

"Why's that?" hollered Katherine.

"Because if this keeps up, the river will swell and overrun its banks."

Katherine cupped her hands and prepared for another shout but the rain let up enough to make it unnecessary. "How often does that happen?"

"Too often," replied Angela. "Trees, cars and even houses get carried away. One time, a flood took out a bridge and a bunch of cars fell into the river."

"You're kidding, right?"

"No. It really happened." Angela moved close enough to the candle to cast ominous shadows across her face. Narrowing her eyes, she spoke in a deep, menacing voice. "But a lot of people say it wasn't caused by a flood."

"Okay," groaned Katherine. "I'll bite. What *really* caused it?"

"Well, the way I hear it, back in the 60s, a lot of good, honest, church-type people out in Point Pleasant started seeing things they couldn't explain. Things like flying objects and weird lightning flashes that lit up the sky but made no noise. Local newspapers talked about UFOs and alien invasions. There was even talk that the people seeing those things were having hallucinations."

"So what's all this got to do with rain?" Katherine reached for the popcorn.

"I'll get to that in a minute. Meanwhile, let me tell the story."

Katherine nodded and stuffed a fist-full of popcorn in her mouth.

"Anyway, when people started complaining about strange lights and noises coming from an abandoned TNT plant out on the Ohio River, the local police force sent a man out to investigate." She raised her root beer float and slowly sipped.

"And . . . and?"

"He never came back."

Katherine braced herself against the table.

"Other things started happening. Kids at the local lovers' lane were chased by what they called a howling monster. An old Indian chief's grave was dug up. Hunting dogs wouldn't hunt. Cows and horses were found disemboweled along the banks of the river. Most of them had their blood sucked dry. TVs turned on and off by themselves and telephones rang but went static when picked up."

Katherine nervously stuffed her mouth with more popcorn.

"The only thing these incidents had in common was that all the witnesses reported seeing an eight-foot-tall bird-like creature. They said it walked like a man and had large, red, mesmerizing eyes and a twelve-foot wingspan."

Katherine's gulp was loud enough to be heard in the next county.

"Whenever someone discovered it, the creature flapped its wings, lifted off from the ground and flew away. Sometimes, like with the kids at the lovers' lane, it followed people. Other times, it flew in the direction of the TNT plant. Since it only came out at night, people started calling it the *Mothman*."

"Can we talk about something else?"

Angela ignored Katherine's plea. "A reporter from one of the local newspapers did some research and found out that there had been a whole series of strange happenings at that TNT plant. Wild plants like ramps and mushrooms grew to enormous size. Sparrows developed eagle-sized talons. Groundhogs became aggressive. The reporter put two and two together and wrote a story theorizing that the creature might have been some sort of mutant created by a gone-wrong chemical experiment and that that was the reason the plant had been abandoned."

Katherine hugged herself and scrunched down.

"During the fall of 1967, West Virginia experienced an abnormal amount of rain. Roads were washed out, trees uprooted, houses destroyed. There had been so much flooding that the DOT sent crews out to inspect all the bridges just to be sure they were safe. A few bridges were shut down but the one over the Ohio River in Point Pleasant passed with flying colors." Angela nibbled on a kernel of corn.

"Then what?" Katherine sounded like she

didn't really want to know.

"On December 15th, a lot of people were hurrying home from work and Christmas shopping when traffic lights on the Ohio side of the bridge malfunctioned. Traffic got backed up on the bridge and everyone started honking their horns and yelling. Suddenly, there was a blinding flash and loud popping sounds and several overhead cables broke loose. Nuts, bolts and cables shattered windshields and smashed car roofs. Without the support of the cables, the bridge started swaying and twisting. Within seconds, a large section broke off. Thirty-one cars went into the river and forty-six souls were lost."

"The Mothman?" It was as much a statement as a question.

"All the newspapers and TV stations claimed it was *undetected structural damage due to recent rain* but almost all the survivors insisted it was Mothman. They believed he was an abomination that dwelled at the TNT plant and only came out at night to seek revenge on the world that created him."

"So what happened? Did they go in there and blast him out?"

"Well, no. They looked for him but never found him. Some people say he went into hiding and that he's still around just waiting for another chance. Or victim."

A rattling at the door startled both women. "What's that?" whispered Katherine.

"I don't know." Fighting the urge to crawl under the coffee table with her dog, Angela reached for Katherine's hand but Katherine was already bolting up the stairs.

"Where are you going?" There was another rattle and Angela blew out the candles.

An eternity later, Katherine stumbled down the steps. "Angela? Where are you?"

"Here," Angela flailed her hand through the darkness to feel for Katherine. What she connected with was cold, hard metal. "Is that a gun?"

"Yes," whispered Katherine. "I brought it for protection."

The front door suddenly opened. A bolt of lightning lit up the sky and revealed the shape of a man standing in the doorway. Gizmo whimpered. Katherine fired. Angela screamed.

The shape shouted. "No. No. It is only me. Gilberto."

Angela ran toward the door. "Gil. Are you all right? Have you been hit?"

"I am fine, *amore mio.* Who is it that shot at me? And why are the lights out?"

"It's Katherine. She just got here today and we were eating popcorn when the lights

250

went out." Feeling for bullet holes, Angela frantically ran her hands over Gilberto's chest and arms.

"Ah, *sì*. The rain. But why did she shoot at me?"

"I thought you were the Mothman," muttered Katherine.

"The what?"

"The Mothman," replied Angela. "It's a long story. I'll tell you about it later. Right now, all I can think about is you. Are you sure you're okay?"

Gilberto wrapped his arms around Angela. "*Sì*, I am all right."

Angela started crying. "What if she'd hit you? What if you'd been hurt? You're my entire life, Gil. How could I go on without you?"

Gilberto hugged his wife tighter. "Don't worry, Angela, I will never leave you . . . ever."

18
THE FESTIVAL

The only thing Angela could think about was that Gilberto was home . . . and safe. Nothing else mattered. Not the farm, not her possible illness, not even seeing him with another woman. After all, what had she *really* seen? Two people holding hands? How serious was that? The previous night's events made her realize how empty her life would be without him. Gilberto meant everything to her. She'd almost lost him in Florida and she was about to lose him here in West Virginia. Katherine said Gil wasn't the type to cheat. Maybe she was right . . . maybe nothing happened . . . maybe she was blowing things out of proportion . . . maybe she should give him another chance. Maybe, maybe, maybe.

Gilberto was in the kitchen making breakfast when Angela came down the stairs. She walked up behind him, hugged his waist and gently laid her head against his back. "I'm so glad you're home, Gil. Are you sure you're all right?"

"*Sì*," he replied. "I am fine. But if you do not let me go, breakfast will be ruined."

Angela released her grip and stepped back. "Smells wonderful. What are you making?"

"A zucchini frittata. Since we have company, I thought it would be a good way to use up some of our garden vegetables."

Angela looked puzzled but quickly remembered. "Oh, you mean Katherine?"

"*Sì*, Katherine."

"She went back to Monica's last night."

"Alone? In the dark?"

"Seems that way." Angela sat at the kitchen table and studied her husband. Even for eighty, he was still a good-looking man. His face was wrinkle-free, his silvery hair was full and there wasn't an ounce of fat on his body. No wonder Gelah was attracted to him. What woman wouldn't be? "I guess she was afraid I might tell another ghost story so she left."

Gilberto pulled a large baking pan out of the oven. Nearly overflowing with eggs, cheese and zucchini, its aroma filled the room. Before closing the oven, he also pulled out a loaf of bread.

"You made bread, too?"

"But of course." Tearing a piece from the loaf, he smiled and handed it to Angela.

Angela dropped the bread and blew on her fingers. "Ouch, that's hot."

Gilberto fell to his knees. "Sono spiacente," he begged. "Non ho significato per dolerla."

Angela raised her eyebrows and laughed. "What?"

"I said I did not mean to hurt you."

Was he apologizing for the bread or something else? Angela shook her head to clear it of negative thoughts. "It's nothing. I'll get over it." *Eventually.*

Gilberto was serving a plate of frittata to Angela when Katherine pranced through the back door. "Well, it's about time you two got up." Spotting the bread and eggs, she sat down at the table and grinned at Gilberto. "I'll have what she's having."

"What's the matter?" asked Angela, "Monica didn't feed you?"

"Yeah, but that was hours ago. You know how I get when I'm not fed regularly."

Gilberto placed a wedge of frittata on a plate, added a few tomato slices and freshly grated parmesan and handed it to Katherine. "Enjoy," he said.

"I intend to." Katherine stuffed a forkful of eggs and cheese in her mouth and followed up with a large bite of bread. "Hmmm. What is it you Italians say? *Deliciosis?*"

Gilberto smirked. "Close enough."

Katherine waved her fork in the air. "Hey, Monica says that big festival thingy starts today. She and Steve aren't going to go until tomorrow. Wanna get a jump on 'em and go today?"

Angela shook her head. "I should probably stick around in case the doctor calls."

"Turn your answering machine on."

"We don't have one," replied Angela.

"Why on earth not?"

"Party line. Remember?"

Katherine rolled her eyes. "That's right. Out here in the boonies you're lucky to even have a phone."

Ever since arriving, Katherine had been ridiculing everything about the farm and country life. It was beginning to wear on Angela's nerves. "It beats smoke signals."

Katherine glared but didn't attempt to top Angela's comeback.

"We should go," declared Gilberto. "I will tell Steve to answer our telephone if it should ring."

"Oh, I don't know," objected Angela.

"It will do us good to spend time with our friends."

"Well . . . maybe you're right." Angela really wanted to stay home and spend a quiet day with Gilberto but she knew she had an obligation to her friends. After all, they would be leaving soon. She and Gilberto would have time enough to talk later.

Katherine jumped from her seat, grabbed the phone and called the main house. "Tell Mongo to get himself up here. Gil's been cooking up a storm and we're getting ready to go to town." She mumbled a few more words then hung up. "He's on his way."

By the time Mongo arrived, all that was left of breakfast were a few crumbs and a sink full of dirty dishes. Eager to get started, everyone was outside, standing around Gilberto's truck and waiting.

"Where have you been?" bellowed Katherine.

"Feeding the rabbits," answered Mongo.

Katherine shook her head in frustration. "Get in the truck."

Mongo obeyed and squirmed into the back seat. Feeling sorry that he had to put up with Katherine's bossy behavior, Angela slid in next to him. Katherine might have been a dear friend but sometimes she went too far.

On the way to town, Katherine tried to make small talk with Gilberto. "So . . . how do you like farm life? Learning all sorts of new and interesting things?"

"*Sì*," replied Gilberto. "Many new things."

"Like what?"

Gilberto shrugged his shoulders. "How to drive a tractor and fix a fence."

"That's it?" Katherine's shrill voice reverberated through the truck. "What about planting crops and taking care of livestock?"

"No," he replied. "Not so much."

"Really? Why not? Too much work?"

"Sì, there is a lot of work."

"Angela told me you went down to Alabama for a couple of days. Did you go to watch them play football?"

Gilberto tightened his grip on the steering wheel but remained silent.

Seeing what was happening, Angela leaned forward and tapped Katherine on the shoulder. "Hey, I hope you brought a lot of money. I hear they're going to have all sorts of furniture and antiques. Someone said they even sold vintage clothing like hats and boas. You might be able to pick up something for the Foxy Ladies."

Katherine turned to face Angela. "Really? If I can find a sunbonnet, I might buy it. Wouldn't I look cute?"

Angela kept the conversation going all the way to town. At one point, she caught a glimpse of Gilberto smiling, probably because he had been rescued from a barrage of incessant questions he didn't want to answer. Questions that Angela wasn't ready to ask.

When they arrived in town, they were directed to park in the Lutheran church parking lot, the same place they'd held the farmers' market earlier in the season. Angela looked around. The vegetable stands were gone, the shoppers were gone but the memories remained. How long ago had that been? Weeks? Months? It seemed like years.

Gilberto helped Angela out of the truck and held her hand as they walked toward the town plaza. Along the way, they passed vendors selling cheap knick-knacks, helium balloons, plastic-wrapped lollipops and t-shirts.

An excessively exuberant salesman beckoned to Gilberto. "Hey mister, wanna buy a watch? I'll make you a good deal." Gilberto shook his head and walked away but Mongo was lured by the man's chutzpa. "How much for that one?" He pointed to a silver and gold watch bearing the name *Rollox*. The salesman beamed. "Ah, you've got a good eye, sir. That's my finest watch. I'll let you have it for fifty bucks." Gilberto shook his head again and dragged Mongo away.

"Maybe we will come back later," he said. The man was already hawking another customer.

When they reached the plaza, they found what they'd come to see — booths decked out in colorful streamers and lacy cloths, food carts selling turkey legs, candy apples and corn dogs, and table after table stacked with homemade jams, jellies, pickles and peaches. The booths, tables and carts lined both sides of all four streets surrounding the plaza. White-haired women wearing calico aprons showed off quilts and shawls they'd spent countless hours creating. Men, some missing fingers, others missing teeth, sat quietly as shoppers scrutinized their handcrafted chairs and tables. There were dancers on a wooden stage, musicians playing dulcimers and violins, and people demonstrating how to blow glass, fire pottery and build birdhouses.

"Wow," Katherine eyes bulged. "Where do you start?"

Angela had been to enough state fairs to know what to do. "Let's check out all the booths on one side of the street and then double back and get the ones on the other side."

"Good thinking," agreed Katherine. Then, spotting a group of women armed with overloaded shopping bags, she pushed her way through the crowd. "Come on. Let's follow them — they look like they've been here a time or two."

Aside from talking to a couple of craftsmen, Mongo and Gilberto lagged behind as their wives perused the booths. After an hour of searching for but not finding a sunbonnet, Katherine suggested stopping for food.

"But you ate before we left," protested Angela. "You can't be hungry again."

"Can't I?" protested the redhead. "Watch this." Katherine walked up to the turkey cart, ordered four barbecued legs, handed three to her friends and bit into the fourth. Next, she bought a bucket of popcorn, four lemonades and one cotton candy. "We'll have to share this," she grumbled, "the cotton candy machine just quit working." Mongo motioned toward an empty picnic table but Katherine refused to stay put. "Come on, there's lots more to see." With turkey leg held high, she forged ahead.

Rounding a corner, Angela spotted Sharon and her daughters standing behind a six-foot long table laden with pink, blue, yellow and green gingham purses, aprons and bonnets. She steered Katherine toward the table. "Is this what you're looking for?"

Sharon leaned over the table and hugged Angela. "I hear'd you was in the hospital. Anythin' serious?" Her face looked fresh-scrubbed and concerned.

"I don't know yet," replied Angela. "But thanks for asking." Fingering one of the purses, she picked it up to get a closer look. "This fabric looks familiar."

"It should," boasted Sharon. "It's the stuff you bought to make the church curtains. Remember? Hope you don't mind me usin' it. It's fer a good cause." She pointed at a sign in the middle of her table. *All proceeds benefit the Wildwood Church of Stringtown.* "It were my girls' idear. Said maybe they could buy a piany or sumppin fer the church. Think the preacher's gonna be vexed?"

Angela rummaged in her purse for money. "He doesn't know?"

Sharon hung her head. "Nope."

A few months ago, this woman was hesitant about letting her children attend Steve's church. Now she was helping them raise money to benefit it. "I'm sure he will be pleased," replied Angela. "In fact, I think he will be *very* pleased."

"How do I look?" Katherine was modeling a pink sunbonnet and strutting back and forth in front of her friends.

"Charming," muttered Mongo.

"You should get two," suggested Angela. "That way you can wear one while the other one's in the wash."

"Boy, you're just full of good ideas." Katherine paid for the bonnet and whispered in Angela's ear as they walked away from the table. "Did you notice those two young girls weren't wearing shoes? What's wrong with these people? The women don't wear makeup, the kids dress like rag-a-muffins and most of the men smell like your goats. Don't hillbillies have any pride?"

Angela stopped dead in her tracks. "You can ridicule my goats and even the house I live in but don't criticize my friends and don't call them hillbillies." She threw her shoulders back and stomped away.

Katherine ran to catch up. "Angela, wait. I didn't mean to upset you."

"Well, you did."

"But didn't you come out here so you could teach these people how to better themselves?"

Angela whipped around and faced Katherine. "The Appalachian people are very proud. They work hard for everything they get, they don't accept charity, and if their kids want to go barefoot in the summer, who cares? They don't have much because they don't need much. They live close to the earth and respect it instead of exploiting it like everyone else. I didn't come here to change anyone, I came here to learn to live like them."

"In poverty?"

"It's not poverty, Katherine. It's called simple living." Angela shouted loud enough to attract the attention of a few shoppers.

"Well, I don't get it."

"Obviously." Angela knew some people didn't understand why anyone would want to live in a rundown house at the end of a backwoods hollow. She knew some people considered farming and living off the land a primitive existence. And she knew some people couldn't live without expensive cars, big houses or fancy restaurants. But she didn't know Katherine was one of those people.

Gilberto and Mongo remained silent and watched as the whole scene unfolded. Katherine stood motionless, her mouth open and her eyes unblinking.

All of a sudden, Angela felt very small. It was as if everything inside her body was shrinking. She couldn't think. She couldn't breathe. Then she looked into her best friend's eyes, the eyes of the woman who would soon be moving away, perhaps never to be seen again. Sure, she and Katherine didn't always agree but differences were what made life interesting. And friendship was what helped people make it through tough times. Katherine came all the way to West Virginia just to be by her side and Angela loved her for it. Knowing she would miss Katherine when she was gone, she broke into tears. "Oh, Katherine. I'm so sorry. I shouldn't have spoken to you that way."

Katherine hugged her. "Hey, you've been through a lot, sweetie. You've got a right to lose it once in a while. Besides, I shouldn't have called your friends hillbillies." She kissed Angela's cheek and dried her tears with one of the bonnets she'd bought. "Now, whaddaya say we forget the whole thing and get back to some serious shopping?"

Angela nodded, Gilberto smiled and Mongo shook his head.

For the next two hours, they checked out the remaining tables and booths. Angela bought two bentwood rockers for her front porch and Katherine bought more food. When they had seen all there was to see, they returned to Gilberto's truck and headed back to the farm.

Steve was raking the garden when the

group arrived. He walked up to the truck and inspected the rockers tied down in the back. "Nice chairs. Did you guys have fun in town?"

"Oh, yeah," chirped Katherine. "But I wanna go back tomorrow. They're gonna have a pig roast and I wanna try it."

"Show him your bonnet," said Angela.

Katherine placed the still-damp bonnet on her head and struck a pose. "Whaddaya think? Will it go over in Cuba?"

Everyone but Mongo laughed. He just shook his head . . . again.

"Did anyone call?" asked Angela.

"Oh, yeah. Doctor Jonas called."

Angela took a deep breath and reached for Gilberto's hand. "And . . . ?"

Steve smiled. "It was good news. The tumor was benign. You don't have cancer, Angela."

Angela closed her eyes, nodded and slowly exhaled. Then she began to cry.

Katherine ran to her side. "What's with you and all the waterworks? Every time I look at you, you're crying." She yanked the bonnet from her head and dabbed at Angela's tears. "Lucky thing I've got this bonnet."

"And lucky thing I've got you as my friend." What would she do without her?

19
THANKSGIVING

With the cancer scare behind her, Angela focused on gluing the pieces of her shattered life together. Starting with the farm, she bounced back into her daily routine of swapping milking and goat grooming duties with Monica. She even helped administer vitamin and antibiotic vaccines so the does would be ready for kidding season. Next, she harvested the remnants of the garden, cooked a huge pot of vegetable soup and delivered it to the widow Putnam and her children in Looneyville. With winter coming, the woman would need all the help she could get. Her most difficult task, however, was forgiving, if not entirely forgetting, that matter with Gelah. Every time she looked at Gilberto, she remembered the whole thing. Even though Gilberto swore nothing happened, he avoided talking about the trip to Alabama. All he ever said was *it was business*. Angela wondered what kind of business drove a man to leave his wife's hospital bed and run off with another woman. True to form, she never asked. Since the night of the storm, Gilberto hadn't left her side. Having him there made everything better.

Shortly after returning to Florida, Katherine and Mongo sold their trailer to a Wall Street broker who wanted to get away from the *Jungle.* Luckily, the deal went through before the housing market hit the skids otherwise they would have been stuck with a sixty-thousand dollar movable house they couldn't drive to Cuba.

Angela had spoken to Katherine before the big move but not since. She'd received a letter saying they found a house on the outskirts of Havana and were adjusting to their new life but the letter didn't say whether they were happy or not. She hoped they were. Thanksgiving was coming up — maybe she would call them then.

The week before Thanksgiving, Tony called and asked if he could spend the holiday in West Virginia. "Fran is going to Biloxi to visit her cousins and I don't see any sense in cooking a whole turkey just for myself. Besides, I haven't seen your place yet. Gotta make sure my baby sister is being taken care of. Whaddaya say?"

Angela suspected there was probably a lot

more to the story, more than she really wanted to know. "Things are going to be pretty busy around here. They're delivering a new church bell on Monday. Steve wants to get it set up and hold a dedication service on Sunday after Thanksgiving." It was a lame excuse but it was the best she could come up with on short notice.

"Don't worry about me, little sister. I'll keep out of the way."

Making a mental list of all the things that could go wrong, Angela hesitated.

"Hey, if you don't want me there, say so."

Tony's icy tone pierced her heart. "Of course I want you here, Tony. It's just I don't know how much time I'll be able to spend with you."

"I can entertain myself," Tony assured her. "Worse comes to worst, I'll play with your goats."

The minute she agreed, Angela wondered what she was letting herself in for. Katherine had mentioned that Tony's drinking was getting out of control and that he was arguing with Fran about rehab. Was he using the trip to get out of going? He had four DUIs. Did the police have a warrant out for his arrest? Would she be accused of harboring a criminal if she took him in? Could she be thrown in jail for a thing like that? If so, would Gilberto come to visit her? She wanted to tell Tony not to come but she didn't. He was her brother and she would stand beside him . . . no matter what.

Tony showed up bright and early on Tuesday morning. Having driven a thousand miles straight through from Florida to West Virginia, he was unshaven and smelled of stale coffee and nacho chips. His eyes were a little bloodshot but Angela told herself that was due to exhaustion. Because the riverside trailer was unheated, she got him settled in her spare bedroom. It wasn't as big as the trailer but it was warm, dry and comfortable. The instant Tony's head hit the pillow, he started snoring. *So much for hello and how are you,* thought Angela.

While Tony slept, Angela went about her chores. Thanksgiving dinner was going to be at Steve and Monica's house but she was in charge of dessert. She'd considered making a black walnut pie, persimmon cheesecake or pumpkin swirl brownies, but unable to decide on just one, ended up choosing all three. That was okay. Everyone loved her desserts and if there were any leftovers, she could take them to the dedication on Sunday.

She had enough black walnuts and chocolate to make the pie and brownies but she still had to go out and pick some wild persimmons for the cheesecake. Knowing everyone else was busy with their own chores, she grabbed her jacket and rattled Gizmo's leash. "Wanna go for a walk, buddy?"

Gizmo was curled up in his usual spot by the front door. When he heard the word *walk* he slowly rose, arched his back and yawned. Angela had noticed the dog was sleeping a lot more since she came back from the hospital. He still got out and ran around with the goats but something was different. It was as if the spark had gone out of him. The vet said it was old age. He was twelve years old. How many more years did he have left? She shook the thought from her head and clipped the leash to the dog's collar. "Come on, boy. Let's go find those persimmons."

It was a perfect autumn morning. The humidity was low, the air was crisp and the sun was shining. The school bus had picked up its passengers earlier in the morning. The children would be home from Wednesday until Monday but for now, the hollow was void of their laughter. Angela missed that.

Leaves crunched under her feet as she and Gizmo made their way into the woods. "I'm not sure what I'm looking for," she told the dog, "but I'll probably know it when I see it." As if off on a great adventure, Gizmo trotted ahead.

Pam told Angela to look for a tall golden tree with golf ball-size fruit lying on the ground. "Depending on how many critters have been around, there might not be a lot of them but at least you'll know they're ripe. Even though we've had our first frost, some of the fruits still on the tree are so green they'll turn your mouth to powder. If you absolutely have to pick them off the tree, make sure they're not hard or bright orange. Soft and brown is best." She also said something about sucking on the seeds and spitting them on the ground so more trees would grow but Angela decided that was something best left for another day.

After walking for half-an-hour, Angela spotted a multi-branched tree loaded with brownish-orange globes. Littering the ground beneath the tree were numerous brown seeds. "Ah ha," she proclaimed, "this must be the place."

The tree looked to be more than twenty feet tall but its heavy branches drooped low enough to the ground to make picking the fruit easy. Luckily, most of them looked ripe. Within minutes, she gathered enough fruit to make the cheesecake and maybe even a few jars of chutney. She stuffed the fruit into her pockets, patted Gizmo's head and started for home when an unusual odor caught her attention. It was the smell of burning wood mixed with . . . what? Something metallic?

Smelling smoke around a house wasn't unusual but smelling it out in the middle of the woods was. What if there was a forest fire? She tried to track the origin of the smell but an erratic breeze carried the scent in several directions at once. "Come on boy, let's check it out."

Angela hustled Gizmo down a well-worn path that cut across the top of the ridge. The further she went, the stronger the smell grew. Looking down, she saw Pam's house but no smoke. That was good. Then Sharon's house. Everything was okay there as well. What if it was one of the old shacks in Stringtown? Or worse, what if it was the church?

As she hurried toward the church, she heard footsteps. Whoever was coming her way didn't seem to be in much of a hurry. Maybe nothing was wrong and that person would know where the smell was coming from.

The footsteps belonged to J.B. "Well, well.

Mrs. Fontero. Whaddaya doin' out cheer all by yourself?" His sneer revealed a blackened tooth. Had it always been that way or was this something new?

"I smelled smoke and wanted to see where it was coming from."

Gizmo lowered his head and uttered a deep-throated growl.

J.B. snickered. "Ain' nuttin' to worry 'bout. I bin burning trash. What? Didya think it were a forest fire or sumppin?"

Angela shook her head. "I didn't know what it was."

"Well, never you mind. I got evry'thin under control."

When Angela got back to the house, she told Gilberto what had happened. "That man scares me."

"Do not be frightened," said Gilberto. "He means you no harm."

Angela wondered how he could be so sure.

Thanksgiving dinner turned into an all day event. Throughout the day, people dropped in to sample Monica's turkey, stuffing and candied sweet potatoes. Some brought side dishes, others just their appetites. Angela's desserts were such a huge success, she worried there wouldn't be enough left for the dedication. Monica assured her they could make a run into town to buy donuts but, somehow, donuts just didn't seem appropriate.

Steve told anyone who would listen about his plans for the dedication. "The children have put together a little play about how they earned money to buy the bell and at the end of the play, we'll ring the bell, sing some songs and maybe even dance."

"On Sunday?" gasped a woman. "I thought that were a sin."

"This is a special Sunday," replied Steve. "I'm sure God will approve."

The woman didn't look convinced.

Although he looked bored, Tony behaved himself. As people came in, he introduced himself, shook hands and attempted to make small talk. Late in the afternoon, Pam and J.B. showed up. As if sensing a kindred spirit, J.B. asked Tony if he ever took a drink.

"Never just one," replied Tony.

The two men walked out the door and jumped into J.B.'s Jeep, where they stayed until Pam was ready to go home. For the next two days, any time Angela wanted to find her brother, all she had to do was look for J.B.

When Sunday rolled around, Angela asked Tony if he was going to attend the dedication.

"Nope. J.B. and I are gonna do sum

splorin'. You know I was never inta all that church stuff."

He was even beginning to sound like J.B.

Later at the church, Steve and Monica stood on the front steps and greeted everyone as they arrived. "We're so glad to see you. Please go inside and enjoy some punch. We'll be starting in a few minutes."

The small church filled quickly. Angela recognized most of the faces but a few were unfamiliar. After some of the children explained that the newcomers were their parents and relatives, she patted Steve on the back. "Looks like you've got yourself a bona-fide parish, preacher man."

Steve smiled. "We've got a parish, Angela, not just me. After all, if it wasn't for your idea about sewing curtains, none of this would have happened."

Angela blushed and bit her lower lip to keep from crying. Gilberto cradled her to his chest.

Steve stepped into the church and clapped his hands. "My wife Monica and I want to thank all of you for coming. Today is a special day not only because we are dedicating the new bell which your children's hard work earned but also because we recently found out that our dear friend Angela has been given a clean bill of health." He put his arm around Angela's shoulders and pulled her in next to him.

Everyone cheered and Angela bit her lip again but this time, the trick didn't work. Tears trickled down her cheeks and ran into the corners of her mouth. They were salty, yet incredibly sweet.

Little Florence tugged on Angela's skirt. "Ya wanna napkin, Miss Angela?" The girl handed her a white linen handkerchief. "It be my mamaw's." A single pink rose was embroidered on one corner.

Grateful she hadn't worn makeup, Angela dabbed her eyes and handed the handkerchief back to the girl. "This handkerchief is beautiful, Florence. Please thank your grandmother for letting me use it."

Florence shook her head. "Mamaw passed last winter. But she won't mind ya keepin' it."

Monica once described these people as being clannish and standoffish. Now that she had been around them for a while, Angela realized the reason they seemed clannish was because they valued family more than casual acquaintances. And as for being standoffish, it was true they were hesitant to let other people into their lives, but that was just because they needed to know they were accepted before they could accept anyone else. They asked for nothing but they gave their all. They worked with her, they cared about her, maybe they even loved her. These people weren't just friends, they were family.

Steve clapped his hands again. "I know we don't have enough seats for everyone, so just make yourselves comfortable and sit wherever there's room. Oh, and how about some of you men give up your seats for the women and older folk."

Several men reluctantly rose from the pews and leaned against the walls. An older woman signaled for a toddler to sit on her lap. Two teenage boys walked around and pulled the curtains closed.

The Camp Gizmo children entered through the main doors and marched to the front of the church. Wearing overalls, plaid shirts and straw hats, they looked like younger versions of their parents. Lining up so that the smallest child was in the front, they began to sing. "Old Camp Gizmo it was fun, e-i-e-i-o. And at this camp, we planted corn, e-i-e-i-o. With a corn seed here, and a corn seed there, here a seed, there a seed, everywhere a big corn seed, Old Camp Gizmo it was fun, e-i-e-i-o." By the time the children reached the third verse, people were clapping and dancing in the aisles.

All of a sudden, someone yelled *Fire.* The children stopped singing and people started running for the doors.

Steve told everyone to remain calm and stay inside while he and Gilberto went outside to see what was happening. It didn't take long to find out. The woods behind the church were on fire and the flames were rapidly spreading. Steve threw open the church doors and shouted for everyone to get out. "There are buckets along the outside walls. Form a line from the church down to the river. We've got to protect the church."

Regardless of age, everyone cooperated. White-haired women worked side-by-side with their grandchildren. Young fathers carried infants on their backs. Teenage boys stood with their mothers. Angela and Gilberto took up positions at the head of the line while Steve and Monica ran back and forth making sure everyone knew what to do.

Flames jumped through the trees and landed on the church roof. A couple of men tried to throw water on the roof but the flames spread. Within seconds, the entire back wall of the old church was burning.

Pam frantically grabbed Steve's arm.

"Have you seen my boys?" Her blouse was torn and there was dirt on her face. "I've looked everywhere but I can't find them."

Steve handed Pam over to Monica and raced into the burning church. The back wall and part of the roof collapsed. Someone screamed. Windows exploded and curtains flailed in the draft until they dissolved into dust. The crowd grew quiet as flames engulfed the front doors. It was as if they were all holding their breath.

"There they are," yelled Angela.

Steve emerged from the burning building with one boy on each arm. The older boy was carrying Little Florence. They all had their heads down except for Florence whose little eyes were the size of grapefruits. Her mouth was gaping and she was staring at something in the distance. Pinned to her shirt was the angel pin she won at Camp Gizmo.

Someone ran up with blankets and wrapped them around the group. Monica brushed ashes from Steve's hair and kissed him while Pam cried and hugged her boys.

Angela lifted Florence from the older boy's arms. "What were you looking at, Sweetheart?"

"The angel," replied the girl. "Cain't ya see him?" She pointed toward the road.

Angela turned and looked but she didn't see an angel. She saw Tony standing motionless and looking on in disbelief. The sun was at his back and illuminated his white t-shirt. That must have been why Florence thought he was an angel. "That's not an angel," said Angela, "that's my brother."

"Not him," argued the girl. "The one behind him."

Angela looked again but still didn't see anything.

Monica heard the whole conversation. She kissed Florence's cheek and touched the angel pin. "Remember when you won this?" she asked.

Florence nodded.

"I told you it was a guardian angel that would help protect you. Maybe that's who you saw."

Florence smiled and nodded again.

Tony approached Angela and Monica. "I am so sorry," he apologized.

Angela didn't want to believe her brother had anything to do with fire but why else would he be apologizing? "For the fire? What did you have to do with it?'

"J.B. and I were in the woods . . . working on his still."

"His still?" screeched Pam. "He almost

killed his own sons with that still. Where is he?"

"I think he ran back to your house."

Pam grabbed her sons and turned toward home.

Angela's face was expressionless. "What happened, Tony?"

"We were drinking and didn't notice the pressure building up in the tank. When it blew, everything around us caught fire. There wasn't anything we could do. I was afraid the fire would head this way so I ran as fast as I could to warn you. But I was too late."

As Angela stared into her brother's eyes, the front wall of the church crashed to the ground and the new bell tumbled down the hill.

20
FROM THE ASHES

Angela sat quietly across the table from her brother. Not feeling up to fussing with breakfast, she'd toasted a few slices of bread and placed a box of granola on the table. Neither she nor Tony had touched the food. Even though she still loved her brother, she no longer trusted him. It was bad enough drinking was ruining his life, now it was affecting the lives of others. She and her friends spent a lot of time and effort getting their little church established. In one careless moment, it was gone. What would he do next?

As if reading her mind, Tony was the first to speak. "I've decided to leave this morning. My bags are packed and I'll take off right after I say goodbye to Steve and Monica."

"That's probably best." Angela picked up a piece of toast, tore off a corner, then laid the bread back on the plate. "Do you want me to pack some sandwiches for the trip?"

Tony shook his head. "No. I'll get something on the road. It'll give me a chance to stretch my legs and do some thinking."

"About what?" asked Angela.

"My life," replied Tony. "Seems I've made a real mess of it."

Angela nodded. There was a time when she would have disagreed with Tony and said things weren't as bad as he thought they were but this time was different. The fire hadn't just been bad, it had been life threatening. What if Steve hadn't gotten to those children in time? The rest of the roof could have caved in and killed them.

"So what are you going to do?" she asked.

Tony looked down at the table and played with his cereal spoon. "I'm gonna go to rehab."

Angela reached across the table and touched her brother's hand. "Really?" Her eyes grew misty.

"Yeah. Fran has been trying to talk me into it for quite a while but I never thought it was necessary. I guess I always figured it was something I could handle by myself. Yesterday proved I was wrong." He curled his fingers around Angela's. "You've always been there for me, Sis. How could I do this to you?"

Angela's tears finally broke loose. "You didn't do anything to me, Tony, you did it to yourself. The only thing Fran and I ever wanted was for you to be happy . . . and safe. Now that you've seen what drinking has done to your life, maybe you'll be able to get away from it."

Tony eyes were dark brown pools of sadness and insecurity. "What if I can't?"

"You can do anything you put your mind to, Tony." Angela rose from her chair and hugged her brother. Even if he didn't succeed, he had at least admitted his problem. That was half the battle. "Now eat your breakfast. You've got a long road ahead of you."

Before he left, Angela and Gilberto accompanied Tony down to Steve and Monica's house. Possibly expecting a lecture, Tony looked surprised when Steve offered to ride with him to Florida. "We didn't have much time to visit last week and it would be kind of nice to see everyone at the park again. Besides, I love road trips."

Tony declined, of course, but agreed to make sure all the park residents had Steve's address. He even suggested getting them to send donations to rebuild the church. His, he said, would be the largest.

Once Tony was on his way, Steve, Monica, Angela and Gilberto drove down to the church to assess the ruins. They were sure it was a total loss but when they left yesterday, everything was still smoking. Maybe something had survived the flames.

When they arrived at the church, a pickup was parked in the lot and a man with a rake was poking at some rubble. The man was J.B.

"What's he doing here?" questioned Monica.

"I don't know," muttered Steve. He climbed out of the truck and hurried toward J.B. "What's going on?" he demanded.

"Jist seein' if I could save anythin'."

Steve's jaw tightened. "Well, this is church property, J.B. You shouldn't even be here." His voice was calm but his words were stern.

J.B. continued to rummage through the charred ruins. "I know," he mumbled. "That's why I called them."

Two pickups pulled into the church lot . . . three more parked out on the road. "We came ta help," shouted Sharon. "Us too," echoed a man from the road.

Everyone worked together. Sharon's girls helped their father unload 2x4s; Pam's boys dragged the bell back up the hill. Widow Putnam returned Angela's soup pot — filled with groundhog stew — and Jasper from the grocery store showed up with six dozen glazed donuts. All the Camp Gizmo children, including Florence and her four older brothers, were also there. It seemed everyone wanted to see the church rebuilt. All, that is, except Gelah. Angela wondered if she'd ever see her again.

By late afternoon, all of the debris had been cleared away and the skeleton of four walls stood in place. Since dark was coming on, many of the workers started drifting toward home.

Angela and Gilberto were helping Steve load several scorched pews into the back of his truck. They were going to take the pews back to the farm to be sanded and stained. Steve noticed J.B. sitting on his truck's tailgate and decided to talk to him.

As Steve approached, J.B. jumped off the tailgate and walked toward the front of the truck.

Steve called out. "Wait up, J.B. I want to talk to you."

J.B. lowered his head as he reached for the driver's side door handle. "Whaddaya want, preacher?"

"I want to say thank you." Steve extended his hand but J.B. ignored the gesture.

"Fer what?"

"For organizing all of this." Steve spread

his arms and motioned toward the remaining trucks and the church. "Because of you, our church will be restored."

J.B. kicked a clump of dirt. "Yeah, well, I was the reason it burnt in the first place. Jist seemed like it fell on me ta rebuild it."

Steve placed a hand on J.B.'s shoulder. "Don't be so hard on yourself. It was an accident."

"Maybe, but if it weren't fer that still, it wood'n'a happened." J.B.'s face was drawn and somber, short red hairs peppered his chin. "But don'cha worry none, I tore that thin' down early this morn'n'."

The glimmer of an idea lit up Steve's eyes. "What are you going to do with the copper tubing?"

J.B. tilted his head as if he hadn't heard correctly.

"The old church didn't have plumbing," explained Steve. "If I could buy that tubing maybe we could use it to put in a bathroom. I'll bet everyone would prefer that to an outhouse. Especially in the winter."

J.B. scratched his cheek. "Wanna barter?"

Steve smiled. "Sure. What do you want in exchange?"

"How 'bout come spring you borrow me one'a your goats? I got a field that needs cleared an' I always hear'd goats was good fer that."

"I'll send the whole herd." Steve extended his hand again. This time, J.B. accepted it.

Angela had been sitting on one of the pews watching as the scene unfurled. "All's well that ends well." She smiled and jumped off the truck.

A serious expression crawled across Gilberto's face. "I think we should go home, Angela. There is something I must tell you."

Angela closed her eyes. The moment she'd been dreading had finally arrived. Gilberto was going to answer all the questions she'd been afraid to ask. Her life was about to change . . . again. Should she stop him? Could she? Did she even want to?

"Should we walk?" she asked.

"Si," he replied. "Let us walk."

Leaving the church, they headed for the river. From there, it would be a short walk to the old trailer where they could get a flashlight to aid them on the climb to the ridge.

Along the way, neither Angela nor Gilberto said a word but the silence was not awkward, it was comforting. A gentle splash indicated an animal was in the water either looking for a late snack or trying to avoid becoming one. A great horned owl hooted in a nearby tree. Angela tried to remember the last time she'd heard that sound. *Ah, yes,* she thought, *it was that first night we stayed in the trailer.* It seemed so long ago. Why couldn't time stand still?

When they arrived at the trailer, Gilberto suggested Angela wait outside while he went in and looked for the flashlight. "No one has been in the trailer for a while. There might be, how do you say . . . *critters?* . . . inside."

The night air was cold and Angela's only protection was the hoodie she'd worn earlier in the day. Sitting in one of the Adirondack chairs, she rubbed her arms to keep warm. It didn't help. It was as if the all the blood in her body had been replaced with ice water. All she wanted was to get this whole thing over with. Maybe then she could figure out what to do with the rest of her life.

Gilberto returned with a flashlight and two blankets. After wrapping one blanket around Angela's arms and the other around her legs, he sat in the empty chair.

"What did you want to tell me, Gilberto?" Angela's tone was formal and measured.

"Do you remember the Sunday Miss Gelah brought you some seed catalogs and then ate breakfast at Steve and Monica's house after the service?"

"Yes . . ."

"Steve had preached about the importance of family that morning and then Miss Gelah told us about her children and the foster children she raised."

"Where is this going, Gil?"

"She needed a ride home, so I drove her. On the way, we talked some more about her children and she told me how foster and adopted children had an underground network that helped them track down their biological parents. That was when I began to wonder — if it worked for the children, could it work the other way around?"

Angela inhaled deeply. Her head was spinning and her stomach was twisting into knots. Had Gilberto done what she'd always been afraid to do?

"Miss Gelah introduced me to some of her children and they introduced me to adopted people they knew and I began the search for your daughter."

"Why didn't you tell me this before?"

"I did not want to get your hopes up."

"Did you find her?"

"Miss Gelah did. That was what she was telling me that day at the diner."

Angela rose from her chair and walked in circles. "Where is she? What's her name? Is she well?"

"Yes, Angela, our daughter is well. Her name is Rebecca Taylor and she operates a migrant farm worker camp in southern Alabama."

"Alabama?" That was where Gilberto had gone while she was in the hospital. Everything was beginning to make sense. "Have you seen her?"

"No. She was away on business when I went down there but I left our address and telephone number with one of her workers. She called while your brother was here. I wanted to tell you sooner but you seemed to have so many other things to think about. Then there was the fire . . ."

"Can I meet her?"

"Yes."

"When?"

"As soon as you want."

Gilberto had not cheated. Tony was going to rehab. Steve's church was going to be rebuilt, even bigger and better than before. And her daughter wanted to see her. Angela remembered Steve once saying that God worked in mysterious ways. She needed to believe that. She needed to have more confidence in His mercy.

Angela and Gilberto fell asleep in the chairs, wrapped in the blankets, holding each other's hand, and listening to the

gentle sounds of the night.
Her life had purpose.

HI EVERYONE,

Many of you have been sending emails and I'd like to take this opportunity to thank each and every one of you. It is reassuring to know that so many readers can relate to my "every day" struggles and adventures. You know, sometimes it's the simple things that make life so interesting. We don't have to climb Mount Everest or build a better mousetrap to bring purpose to our lives and we don't need to worry about what tomorrow will bring. All we need to do is keep smiles on our faces, love in our hearts and rely on Him to keep us on the right path. Thanks also for saying you enjoy reading something that isn't filled with four letter words, violence and overt sex. There's enough of that on the TV and movie screens — we don't need to fill another book with it.

As you probably already know from my website, Margaret has begun work on our third book, *Mariposa Landing*. In case you haven't noticed, the theme of all three books is joy, hope and new beginnings. And, since that's what butterflies symbolize, it's appropriate we use the Spanish word for butterfly (Mariposa) in the title — you'll see why once you read it. In this final book of the series, I'll have a brand new and very joyful adventure; I'll be surrounded by lots of old and new friends; and, of course, Gizmo and Gilberto will be along to share in my journey.

Speaking of Gilberto, some of you expressed an interest in his recipes so here are two of them, plus one of my own. They're really easy to make and very delicious. Give them a try and let me know what you think.

OSSO BUCO (OR OSSO BUCCO)

5–6 veal shanks (crosscut into 3-inch pieces
  & tied together with string)
1/4 cup flour
1 tsp sea salt
1/4 tsp freshly ground pepper
3 Tbl butter
3 Tbl extra virgin olive oil
1 medium onion-chopped
1 large carrot-thinly sliced
1/2 cup diced celery
2–4 cloves garlic-crushed
12 oz whole tomatoes
1-cup dry white wine
1 tsp dried basil leaves
1 tsp dried thyme leaves
1 bay leaf
1 Tbl grated lemon peel
chopped parsley

Combine flour, salt and pepper and coat

veal shanks with mixture.

Heat butter and oil in a 5-quart Dutch oven or large skillet and brown veal shanks (3 at a time) over a medium heat for about 30 minutes. Turn frequently to brown all sides, remove as browned and continue with remaining shanks.

Add the onion, carrot, celery and garlic to the drippings in the oven or skillet. Sauté until onion is tender (about 5 minutes), add the tomatoes, wine and seasonings and bring mixture to a boil.

Reduce the heat, add the browned veal shanks (marrow side up), cover and simmer for 2–3 hours or place in a slow cooker for 8–12 hours until meat is very tender. Cool quickly, cover and refrigerate overnight.

To serve: Gently reheat; remove strings; place veal shanks on a warm serving dish. Spoon some of the sauce over the shanks and pass the rest. Garnish with chopped parsley and lemon zest. Serve over saffron risotto or fried polenta.

ZUCCHINI FRITTATA

1/4 cup extra virgin olive oil
1 small onion finely chopped
1 clove garlic minced
3 small zucchini peeled and shredded
6 large eggs

2 Tbl heavy cream
1 cup grated parmesan or Swiss cheese
1/4 tsp sea salt
1/2 tsp freshly ground black pepper
2 Tbl minced parsley, basil or thyme

Heat olive oil in a 10-inch ovenproof skillet. Sauté onions until translucent. Add garlic and zucchini and cook for 5–6 minutes.

Whisk eggs and cream together in a large bowl. Add cheese and herbs and pour over cooked vegetables. Do not stir. Reduce heat and cook 5–6 minutes until bottom of egg mix is golden brown and top is beginning to set.

Transfer pan to oven broiler and brown for 2 minutes or flip frittata over in skillet and brown opposite side.

Slide cooked frittata out of the skillet onto a serving plate and serve with thick slices of crispy Italian bread.